D1095839

Hellbox

HELLBOX

John O'Hara

Random House · New York

FIRST PRINTING

Most of the stories in this book originally appeared
in *The New Yorker*

Published in New York by Random House, Inc., and
simultaneously in Toronto, Canada, by Random House
of Canada, Limited, 1947

Manufactured in the United States of America by
H. Wolff, New York. Designed by Stefan Salter

To Wylie O'Hara

FROM HER FATHER

Contents

Hellbox

There were five in the party, and when they had been seated, the proprietor came over to their table. He nodded to the two girls and to two of the men, none of whose names he knew, although the girls spoke to him by name. Then he said to the third man, "Glad to see you in Chicago, Mr. Spring. Gonna be with us a while, I hope."

"Hello, Mike," said Mr. Spring. He shook hands without standing up. "No, I'm on my way back to the Coast. Just staying overnight."

"Whenner you gonna stay over a couple days again? Like to throw a little party for you again. Remember that one six or seven years ago? In nineteen-and-thirty-nine, I think it was."

"Indeed I do remember it. I'll never forget it. But those days are gone forever, I'm afraid."

"Not for you, Mr. Spring," said Mike. He leaned over and whispered in Spring's ear. "If you see anything in the show you like I'll be glad to fix it up for you."

"Thanks, Mike. I'll let you know. Uh, you know all these people? This is Harry Field, charge of publicity on the Coast, and this is Jake Coombs, my trainer, and I forget the young ladies' names."

"Betty Donaldson," said Betty Donaldson. "Hello, Mike."

"Audrey French," said Audrey French. "Hello, Mike."

"Oh, I've known Mike for years," said Harry Field. "I very seldom pass through Chicago without dropping in."

"That's right," said Mike. "Well, enjoy yourselves, Mr. Spring." He left them, stopping to speak to the maître-dee and at two or three tables, obviously explaining to the people at the tables that Mr. Spring was Mr. Spring, the famous Hollywood producer, an old friend, on his way back to the Coast with his press agent and trainer. The pretty girls were Chicago girls.

The floor show had not started and the relief band was at work. "You people dance if you feel like it," said Mr. Spring.

"Don't you want to, Mr. Spring?" said Field.

"Not right away," said Mr. Spring. His four companions got up and Mr. Spring was alone, practically the first time he had been alone in the two days since he had left Johns Hopkins. He took out a cigar from a case which had been given him by an ex-President of the United States. He replaced the case in the coat of a suit which he had bought from Eddie Schmidt. He snipped off the end of the cigar with a gold cigar cutter which an English actor had bought for him at Asprey's, and lit the cigar with a gold lighter-and-watch which he could not with any certainty ever have identified, since he possessed at least twenty exactly like it. He got a good light and then remembered the orders of the men at Johns Hopkins. "You'd better limit yourself to two a day, Mr. Spring," one man had said. "None at all, if you can do without them. No brandy. No golf. I don't want you to drive a car or gamble or run upstairs, and try to keep your temper and don't get in quarrels with people. No more making speeches."

"You don't leave me much. What about women?"

The doctor had smiled. "From my information, Mr. Spring, you're going to go right on doing as you please about women, but common sense should tell you . . ."

"What if I ignored everything you tell me?"

"Then one of these days you'll feel as if somebody had given you a good swift kick all over the whole left side of your body."

"How long'll that last?"

"I don't know. You might lose your eyesight, too."

"How long'll I last if I *take* your advice?" Mr. Spring had asked.

The doctor had hesitated. "As a rule, I give an evasive answer to that one, but with you I don't think I have to. Take care of yourself, and you have between five and ten years more."

"It hardly seems worth it, does it?"

The doctor had been slightly shocked and annoyed. "I don't know why not. A lot of people that come here would be glad of your chance."

"You're a Catholic, aren't you, Doctor? I never been able to understand how a Catholic can be a good doctor or a good doctor can be a Catholic. Notwithstanding a lot of them are."

"Well, we haven't got time to go into that now, Mr. Spring. I have other patients waiting."

"I beg pardon, Doctor." It was not often that Mr. Spring was put in his place.

He let the cigar go out, resting the lighted end in the ashtray. He watched the dancers with no interest and hummed with the music. When his companions returned he put his right hand on the back of the chair to his right, then put his left hand on the back of the chair to his left. This served as a substitute for standing up for the young ladies. Betty and Audrey looked at him, waiting for him to say something.

"Enjoy your dance?" he said.

They said they had, and he nodded with solemn approval, putting across the further idea that he didn't feel like talking, whereupon Harry and Jake reopened their conversations with the girls. Almost immediately the floor show started.

It was awful. It hadn't been good to begin with, but tonight everyone played with the knowledge that Mr. Spring was at Table 12. In case anyone didn't know the location of Table 12, it was the table behind which stood a captain and two waiters, and if people to the rear could not see through the captain and waiters, that was too bad.

The chorus came out, bumping into each other and generally lousing up the routine in their eagerness to smile for Mr. Spring. The master of ceremonies trotted out to the microphone and tried hard not to look in Mr. Spring's direction, but before he was halfway through his song he was looking nowhere else. Zita and Leonardo, the society dancers, kept to Mr. Spring's side of the floor, and Leonardo almost dropped Zita during a spin. The chorus and the showgirls came out again and got in each other's way; Patsy Whitney, who did imitations, became confused at finding herself started on a rather mean imitation of one of Mr. Spring's stars after Mike had distinctly told her to leave it out tonight; Bobby Renwick, the harmonica player, came right over and stood at the edge of the floor and played Gershwin, Grieg, Arlen, Brahms, and Ravel for a table two removed from Mr. Spring's, an error attributable to Bobby's nearsightedness. It all came to some kind of climax during the finale, when one chorus girl was sent into such a bad fall that the other girls had to dance around her while she was getting to her feet. The other girls grinned, but the one little girl cried, got out of the line, and ran off.

"Harry," said Mr. Spring.

"Yes, Mr. Spring." Harry, Jake, Audrey, and Betty turned to Mr. Spring, and the captain and waiters behind him leaned forward.

"Just Harry," said Mr. Spring to his companions. He whispered in Harry's ear. "Tell Mike I want to see him."

Harry got up from the table, and when he came back Mike was with him. "Here he is," said Harry.

"Yes, I know," said Mr. Spring. "Mike, who's the little girl took the spill?"

Mike leaned down and put a hand on Mr. Spring's shoulder. "Her name is Zita. Zita and Leonardo. I got them out of a hotel in Detroit."

"I don't mean her," said Mr. Spring. "She's all right, but a dime a dozen, Mike. *You* know that. I mean the chorus kid. The number they just finished."

"Oh. She's—I think her name is—" Mike halted and whispered to the captain of waiters, who whispered back. Mike nodded and continued. "Goes by the name of Hilary Kingston. You like her?"

"I might," said Mr. Spring. His companions drank their champagne and tried to pick up their talk where they had left off and to keep talking until the arrival of Hilary Kingston. In a few moments she was there. With a flat-palm gesture, like someone testing a mattress, Mr. Spring bade Harry and Jake and the girls to remain seated. He rose. He put out his hand. "Are you all right, Hilary?" he said. "Sit here next to me." She sat on the chair only just vacated by Audrey, who remained standing while a waiter brought another chair.

"Thanks," said Hilary Kingston. She folded her hands in her lap.

"Did you get hurt? I mean when you fell that time?" asked Mr. Spring.

"No, sir. Not when I fell. I think one of the kids kicked me here, but I can take it," said Hilary. She was wearing a flannel suit and she indicated a slit in the coat where a pocket might have been.

Mr. Spring sternly did not lower his eyes to the place indicated. He smiled. "I was worried for you. It reminded me of when a jockey's thrown in a horse race and I can't look at anything else only him till I see the other horses are safely past him, Hilary. Even when I have a horse running in that particular race. I always shut my eyes to everything else. That can be awful, you know."

"Yes, I know," she said.

"Do you like horse racing, Hilary?"

"Like them? Love them is more the word. This Jake. Is he your trainer?"

Mr. Spring smiled. "If you mean does he train my horses, no. He trains *me*. I have a workout with him every day, boxing, road work, massaging. No, you're thinking of Jock, not Jake. Jock Doyle. He trains my horses, Hilary. But I'm glad to see you have an interest in horse racing. That means two things we have in common. You said you can take it, and so can I. And you like horse racing."

"If I could be a boy, that's what I'd be," said Hilary.

"What?" asked Mr. Spring.

"A jockey."

"Well, just let me say I prefer you the way you are." Mr. Spring smiled.

"Thanks."

Mr. Spring smiled directly at Hilary, straight in the eye and then at the place in her coat where she had thought she might have been kicked. "Did you ever know Harry before?"

"Harry who?"

"Well, if you don't know Harry who, then you didn't. Mr. Field, the handsome gentleman in the blue suit."

"Oh, I don't think he's so handsome," said Hilary.

"You don't? He's considered a very good-looking man, I've always heard."

"Oh, I have nothing against him."

"Very nice fellow to be with and a very good host," said Mr. Spring.

"I thought he worked for you."

"He works for the same company, but when we're out like this, it isn't any question of working for me. All I can say is I'm glad he brought me here. You can see I'm not *with* anybody, Hilary. At least not till you so kindly joined us. Harry's having a party a little later. Would you like to go with me? I'm sure it'll be all right with Mike. I've known Mike since probably before you were born."

"I was born in 1927."

"Oh, is that so?" said Mr. Spring. He leaned forward and spoke to Harry. "Harry, I have a new recruit for your party back at the suite."

"What's that, Mr. Spring?" said Harry.

"I said I persuaded Miss Kingston to join your little party back at the suite," said Mr. Spring. He turned back to Hilary. "If you think there'll be any trouble about you doing another show, I can speak to Mike."

"That's all right, Mr. Spring. That was the last show. We don't do any more."

"Well, that's fine. Then we can go to Harry's party. Harry, whenever you're ready, we are."

"Right," said Harry, signalling to the captain.

Mr. Spring was smiling. He leaned toward Hilary. "We don't have to all go in the same car if you prefer," he said.

"I don't care," said Hilary.

Mr. Spring raised his head. "Harry, Miss Kingston and I will go in the black car and meet you there, if that's all right."

"Right," said Harry.

Mr. Spring smiled, took out a special Upmann cigar from the ex-President's case, snipped off the end with the English actor's Asprey cutter, and put the cigar in his mouth. Then the smiling corners of his mouth turned down for the lighting of the cigar, and he remembered who had given him the cigar case and the cigar cutter and, more clearly, he remembered the words of the doctor in Baltimore. He snapped the lighter shut and turned to Hilary.

"Maybe you don't want to go on this party," he said. He hoped she would say no, but he knew she would say yes.

Pardner

The dashboard clock told him it was too late to stop for something to eat at the Bond, but Malloy recalled from long before the war that there was a good diner just before you came into Hartford. It was a favorite spot of truckmen and served a good beef stew and the apple pie was good, too. But either he passed it while concentrating on his driving or the place no longer existed. In any case, he did not see it, and he decided to stop at the first place on the right-hand side of the road, eat a sandwich, and be on his way. He could get a good meal in New York, and a sandwich and cup of coffee were probably a better idea now, anyway; enough to keep him awake, not so much that he would get drowsy on the Parkway.

The place he chose turned out to be a real restaurant, not de-luxe, but it had a small bar as well as tables and the inevitable juke box. There was room to park right in front of the entrance. When he went in, a party of four were sitting in the rear of the room; the only other persons in evidence were the barkeep, two waitresses, and a boy who appeared to be of high-school age. As Malloy went to a table, the boy went to the front door and stared out at Malloy's car. Malloy gave his order to a waitress and the boy came to Malloy's table.

"I see you got a Doozy," said the boy.

"That's right," said Malloy.

"What year is it?"

"Built in thirty-two," said Malloy.

"Thirty-*two?* Fifteen years ago!"

"That's the way it adds up. Or subtracts," said Malloy.

"What is it, sixteen cylinders?"

"Eight," said Malloy.

"All right if I sit down a minute?" said the boy.

It was not all right, but there was no use making a point of it, and Malloy told the boy to sit down if he liked. The boy was not a standard type, but Malloy foresaw ten minutes of boredom while he answered the same old questions about the Duesenberg. The kid was rather short and very pale, and made Malloy think of the old term, momma's boy. His clothes were awful: a dark-brown double-breasted suit, brown leather-and-suede shoes, chocolate-colored shirt, and plain white four-in-hand tie. He wore a wristwatch with large, square, gold-looking links for a band and on the little finger of his left hand a ring with a large black stone surmounted by a large gold letter "C." On the little finger of the right hand, he wore some kind of school ring. His tie clasp, which he wore high, contained an ornament that may have been inspired by those Longhorn heads with which Frederic Remington used to clutter up his drawings. Finally, he wore a dark-brown hat, which he kept shifting, but which he at no time removed. He could probably run fifty balls in a game of straight pool.

"Can I buy you a drink?" the boy asked.

Malloy controlled the instinct to slap the kid's face. "No, thanks," he said.

"That makes sense," said the kid. "Driving a load of power like that there, a person's better off without any booze in him."

"Right," said Malloy. He realized that the kid was not patronizing him, only treating him as an equal, and he nodded solemnly.

"What's the fastest you ever had it up to?"

"A hundred and five."

The kid nodded approvingly, and Malloy was sorry he had not made it a hundred and twenty, just to see what the reaction would be.

"How many carburetors you got on her?"

"One," said Malloy.

"One. Did you ever stop to think of what you could do with three more?"

"No. A hundred and five's good enough for me."

The kid nodded, like saying, "Yes, at your age."

The waitress brought the sandwich and coffee.

"The usual, M'rie," the kid said. "You sure you won't have something?"

"Positive," said Malloy, and began to eat. The waitress, who obviously loathed the kid, brought the usual.

"Bourbon and 7-Up," said the kid. "You'd like it, or maybe you never heard of it."

"Heard of it," said Malloy, chewing. "You must have a drag here."

"Why? Because I can get a drink at my age?"

"Uh-huh."

"Christ, man, I own the joint."

"You what?"

"You heard me. It was left to me by my old man. My mother's trustee, and I don't get the full control of it till I'm twenty-one, but her and the bank do what I tell them to. The bank knows I know how to make a beautiful buck out of the joint, and they don't bother me, either. Hey, M'rie, bring me a fistful of nickels outa the till." This she did and he held out his hand for them without looking at her. She poured them in his hand instead of throwing them in his face. "Give the party on Four drinks on me, and then you can go home."

"Thanks," said M'rie.

"We'll have a little music," said the kid. "They say it promotes the digestive juices. I happen to like Spike Cooley, the King of Western Swing. Ever hear of him?"

"I don't think so," said Malloy. "The King of *Western* Swing? Where does that leave Benny Goodman?"

"B. G. went out with the horse and carriage for my dough. I don't have one of The Eye's platters in my joint. I turned them over to the U.S.O." He took a gulp of his usual. He nodded in agreement with himself. "Yes sir, Western swing's the coming thing. Say!"

"What?"

"I just gave them a slogan—Western swing's the coming thing. Well, it is. I like it. I like it. Have you ever been out West?"

"Uh-huh."

"Ranching?"

"In a way." Malloy had done his ranching in the writers' annex at Paramount.

"What's it like?"

"Well, it's hard to put into words. Sleeping under the stars. The old chuck wagon comes along about once a week. It's the only life."

"Yeah? How'd you happen to leave it?"

"Well, two reasons. It's awful lonesome out there under the stars. Peaceful, but lonesome, and I used to miss my wife, and she used to miss me, so I got a job in town, and then I ran into a little luck. A gusher came in on the south forty." By now, Malloy was getting carried away with his fiction.

"Oil?"

"Yep. That meant I didn't have to work any more, and Sallie Lou and the kids could have all the advantages. We moved to the city."

"New York?"

"That's where we live now. No, I meant Abilene. Abilene, Texas. Population, 18,000. That was city to us in those days."

"But I'll bet you miss it, living on the ranch."

"It's in my blood. Oh, I still go out every year for round-up time. I got about four thousand head on the home ranch. Longhorns. I noticed you have the head of a Longhorn on that thing in your tie."

"That's not all I got. Take a look at this." The kid stood up and unbuttoned his coat to show his belt—hand-tooled leather with a silver buckle. "That cost me sixteen-fifty. I sent for it out to a place in Pendleton, Oregon."

"Oh, yes. I have some beauties like that. I have a Mexican named Pablo on the home ranch. I guess there isn't a better leather man in Deaf Smith County."

"Death Smith County?"

"Deaf. D-e-a-f. Maybe you pronounce it deef."

"That's a funny name for a county."

"You wouldn't say that out home. Deaf Smith was Vice-President of the old Texas Republic. Stone-deaf. Deaf as a hitching post, but to make up for it he could see in the dark, sharper than a coyote. They tell a lot of stories about him in that connection. I wish I had time. I'd tell you some'd curl your hair."

"You going right back to New York tonight, huh?"

"Yep. Stockholders' meeting in the morning. My oil company."

The kid smiled. "I just figured out something. See if I'm right. The Doozy, I'll bet you bought that when you struck it rich."

"Right on the nose! First, I bought the property in Abilene, then I said to myself I was going to have the biggest, longest, loudest, fastest automobile in West Texas, and out there she is. First automobile I ever owned. I guess I owned a hundred since then, but I held on to that son-of-a-gun out of sentiment. Sallie Lou keeps prodding me, why don't I get rid of that old thing. She won't ride in it. She got a couple Rolls-Royces, but I say to her, 'That's our lucky car. If the wells give out, maybe we'll be lucky to have the one we started with.' "

The kid nodded slowly, in complete approval of the sentiments. He jingled the nickels that he still held in his palm, and at the sound he looked down at them. "Funny you never heard of Spike Cooley. He's known as the King of Western Swing."

"Why, that nothing against him. Nothing against me either, son. The West is a mighty big place, mighty big. The only objection I have, I wish your friend didn't call himself the King. No man—no matter how big he is—no one man's big enough to call himself king of anything in the West, except we have the King Ranch, but that's a different proposition altogether. That's the name of the family who own it and they have a right to call it King Ranch. They would anyhow, even if their name wasn't King, cause that ranch is the king of 'em all. You could put my measly a hundred and forty thousand acres in the King Ranch and all they'd do'd be to use it for a corral, that's how big the King Ranch is." Malloy started to rise.

"Have another sandwich. There wasn't much to that," said the kid.

"Thanks very kindly, but I have to mosey along. I don't want to keep Sallie Lou waiting up for me." He looked around for the other waitress. "Say, Miss," he said.

The kid shook his head no, and the waitress shook her head no, questioningly. "No check," said the kid.

"Oh, now, thanks very kindly, but I insist. I like to pay my own way."

"Maybe some time, maybe next year I'll be out in your country and I can stop at your ranch. How about that?"

"Fine, fine. But let me leave something for the girl," said Malloy.

"Sure, if you want to," said the kid. As Malloy laid a dollar bill on the table, he noticed that something was troubling the kid.

"Something bother you, son?"

"Well, if I did go out there next year—I know you're not supposed to ask a stranger's name . . ."

"Oh. My name. Humber Phillips," said Malloy.

"Humber Phillips. Abilene, Texas. Right." The kid smiled and walked to the door with Malloy. They shook hands, and Malloy, in the car, could see the kid standing in the open doorway, with his coat open and his thumbs in the cowboy belt. Malloy waved to him as the car began to move, and the kid tipped the brim of his hat. "So long, pardner," he heard the kid call out.

Someone to Trust

Tommy stood in the darkened doorway of a band-instrument shop, closed for the night. It was diagonally across the street from the stage door to a theatre, and the stage door was not on the same street as the main entrance. He was glad it was not the cops whom he was avoiding. If it had been the cops, they probably would have gone back a few years and found out about Maida. Plenty of people he knew would have been glad to tell the cops about Maida or be helpful in any other way. As a matter of fact, the same people would be glad to be helpful to the people he was avoiding, if they knew how to be helpful. Tommy faced it: he was not a popular fellow, and he knew he was taking some chances with Maida, but they were chances he had to take or else give up. One chance he was taking—a very serious one—was that Maida might be walking to the theatre with someone who knew him, and that wouldn't be so good. Any friend of Maida's would pull her away as soon as he showed himself. "Don't have anything to do with that louse," the friend would say. If he had time to spare, he could wait until he saw Maida alone and then talk to her, but he had no time to spare. He had to go somewhere tonight, had to have a place to stay tonight, and Maida was his best bet, if not his only bet.

Two girls he knew passed the darkened doorway and proceeded to the theatre. One of them certainly would have turned him in if she had known how, and, come to think of it, Carina *would* have known how. She would have gone straight to her friends up the street and spread the word: "I saw Tommy Welting tonight, if anybody's innarested," and it would not be long before the word did get to an interested party.

Some more girls, obviously from Maida's show, passed the doorway and on to the theatre. He hoped, not exactly for her sake, that nothing had happened to Maida, who was always punctual, the stage manager's delight. He knew for a fact she was in the show; he had seen her pictures and her name in the captions in a picture-magazine layout, less than two weeks before. Even granting the layout did not appear until a month or so after the pictures were taken . . . There she was, and, thank Christ, alone.

He waited until she was almost directly across the street. He didn't want to risk being seen any more than necessary. He hurried over just under a run, and spoke her name, sharply and once. She stopped. She must have recognized his voice.

"Tommy!"

"Yes, honey. Meet me at Fifty-first and Lexington after the show. Fifty-first and Lexington. Southeast corner."

"I can't. I—"

"Life or *death*, honey. Fifty-first and Lexington. Southeast corner."

He recrossed the street and walked west without waiting for any more words from her. As he walked, he congratulated himself on his instinctive choice of words "Honey."

The repeated "honey." The repeated address of the rendez-vous. The emphasis on death. That last would keep her mouth shut, keep her from discussing him with the two girls he knew, especially that one bitch. He went all the way to Fiftieth and Ninth Avenue, got a crosstown bus, and put in the time at a couple of East Side newsreels. He stayed in one of the theatres until Maida's show break and then walked slowly to the vicinity of Fifty-first and Lexington. He bought a couple of papers and took up a position half a block away, so that he could see Maida before she saw him, and, what was of principal importance, to see that she came alone. One of the pansies who abound in that neighborhood tried to pick him up and he wanted to kill the queen; a fine time to tangle with one o*f them*. But he smiled and said, "Not tonight, dear," and the pansy went away.

Tommy saw Maida get out of a taxi, in which she was the only passenger, and cross the street opposite Loew's Lexington. He waited to see that there was no taxi following her and then joined her. "Thanks, honey. We'll go to a bar up the street, where we can talk."

He had cased the joint on his way to meet her and it was not a place where he would be likely to run into anyone he knew. It was really a cheap restaurant that turned into a saloon at night. It would not attract the Broadway mob who wandered over to Third Avenue. It was safe.

They sat in a booth. "A Cuba libre for the lady. A bourbon-and-water for me."

She relaxed a little. "You remembered that, huh?" she said.

"Oh, and, waiter, that's with crushed ice in the Cuba libre," he said. "Sure I remember." He did not bother to tell her that he had been trying to remember all through the newsreels and had not remembered until the second running of a newsreel clip about Cuba. "*You* didn't remember something, though."

"What? You mean the southeast corner?"

"You hit it."

"You're right. I couldn't remember was it southeast or southwest."

"Or maybe you remembered it was southeast but you went over to the southwest to get a look at me."

"Maybe," she said. "What's it all about, Tommy? That stuff about life and death . . ."

"Before I answer that, did you mention you saw me to anybody? Anybody at all?"

"No. I almost did. Carina's in the show and I almost said something to her, but I decided I wouldn't," said Maida.

"Thank God you didn't, honey," said Tommy. The drinks came and they touched glasses. "Here's to some of the good times."

"Yes. We had some," she said.

"You *know* we did," he said, and drank. He put down his glass and pulled out a half-empty pack of Luckies and an unopened pack of Camels, which he pushed toward her.

"You remembered that, too," she said.

"Sure. Shall I open them the way you open 'em? I always louse it up, but I could show you I remember."

"I'll do it," she said, but he knew he had got to her better than if he had sent her fifty bucks' worth of flowers.

"I never forget anything, honey, and that's why when I'm in a jam I come to you," he said.

"You look as if you were right up there. Of course, you were always one for the wardrobe, but I'll bet those threads came from a tailor."

"It isn't a money jam, honey," he said. "Or at least I have enough scratch so I don't have to put the bee on you or anybody else."

"What kind of a jam is it?"

"First, I have to ask you a couple questions. Are you shacked up with anybody now?"

"Not exactly," she said.

"How do you mean not exactly?"

"Well, *shacked up*. There's somebody wants me to marry him and I guess I will."

"You don't sound as if you loved him," he said.

"It's a year and a half—that's longer than us two were," she said.

"Are you living with *him?*"

"About the way I was with you. Sometimes I go to his place, sometimes he comes over to mine."

"You still got the same place?" he asked.

"Oh, sure. I never had any trouble. They never threatened to kick me out or raise the rent or you know—like make a phony bet and pay extra that way, the way some of the kids I know had to. One kid in the show, every week she bet the manager of her hotel, like he'd bet her ten dollars every week she didn't know what his middle name was, or where he was born. That was the only way she could keep her room. But where I am they were always decent to me, I guess because I'm a regular fixture there."

"Well, they like you," he said.

"Yes, I guess they do. How could they help it, ha, ha, ha!"

"You don't have to kid about that. Everybody likes you, honey."

"A few do," she said.

"If *I* do?"

"No, I said a few do," she said.

"Oh."

There was a moment's silence.

"What's the jam, Tommy?"

"It's a jam. I wasn't exaggerating. It's a matter of life and death, but I don't know how much to tell you. This other guy you got now."

"Well, never mind about him for now. What do you want *me* to do?"

"*I* can't say never mind about him. Who *is* he?" he asked. "Not a musician, I hope."

"No. But he's in show business. He has a bit." She named a musical comedy. "Harry Trent."

"Oh, yeah. I saw his name some place," he said. "I don't know him."

"I know you don't," she said.

"Why? Did you ask him?"

"He knows you and I used to go around together," she said. "He doesn't mind what happened before I knew him."

"He oughta mind. It's something he'll never have, or any-one else."

"I'm gonna meet him later, Tommy, so you better tell me what you want."

"Let's have another drink, honey. And you meet Harry." He called the waiter and reordered. They studied each other while the drinks were coming, and Tommy wished he could tell her to go to hell. She had not lost her prettiness, she looked no older, but for a year and a half she had been sleeping with someone else, meeting him, eating with him, exchanging Christmas presents, talking about jobs, getting sore at one another, making up. It made her kind of a bum, where Carina, who didn't keep with one man longer than three weeks, wasn't a bum. Much as he wanted to tell her to go to hell, he couldn't. She was the only person in New York, and, as far as he could think of, in the whole world, that he could possibly count on. The drinks were served. Before she picked up her glass, she looked at her watch. He saw it was time to make the big pitch, if he only knew what kind of a pitch to make.

"I want to help you if I can, Tommy," she said.

"Honey, I don't want you to take this the wrong way, but I don't think I can trust you," he said. "I just got in town to-day, and you were the only person I could think of. That I could trust. I'm hot, kid."

"You mean you're mixed up with mobsters?"

"Mixed up like a thirty-cent hash. Like mincemeat. That's what I'll be if I run into any of them. That's why I'm glad you didn't pipe to Carina. She knows too many of those characters and she don't like Mr. Tommy, and when you leave me to meet Harry, do me one last favor. Forget you saw me. Forget you even remembered I ever lived. If anybody asks about me, all you say is 'Who's he?' I'm doing you a favor by not telling you any more about myself. That way, you don't know anything in case anybody should ask you."

"What was it—liquor?"

"No, the Eyeties are back in that. That's what we called them in the Army. The Eyeties. No, it was something else. Give yourself a break and don't load up on information. The deal I was in, I held out a little, only they didn't think it was a *little*. They took care of the guy that I was cutting it up with."

"They killed him?"

He waited before speaking, and suddenly—looking at her closing eyelids and seeing the excitement building—he remembered things about her and he knew how to handle her. It was going to be easy; he had only to tell her the truth.

"Yeah. Finally, they killed him. *Finally*. I was to meet him at my apartment and I was late, but *they* weren't, and I heard him let out a coupla screams. I don't have to tell you I didn't stop and collect the rest of my wardrobe. I got a ride on a truck to another town and from there I rode the airplanes—the short hops, not like T.W.A. or those. I got to Washington, D. C., and took the rattler there as far as Trenton, New Jersey, and thumbed it in the rest of the way here. I only got in about an hour before I saw you tonight."

"Christ, you *are* hot!" she said. It was a whisper.

"Me and that two-dollar pistol," he said.

"What two-dollar pistol?"

"That's an old saying. As hot as a two-dollar pistol."

"Oh, I thought maybe you had a two-dollar pistol or something," she said.

He took another chance to keep up her mood. "Not a two-dollar one, honey. Sixty, the one I have. What they call the difference. The difference between me and somebody that don't happen to have one on him. And it's gotta be good, because it's all I got, honey. *Money* I got, but money ain't what'll stop *my* chums." He was on the verge of telling her to drink up, but immediately he realized that would have been a mistake. She put her right hand on her left shoulder without successfully hiding the deep, full breathing.

"I get it," she said quietly. "I'm to be your hideout."

"Mm-hmm."

"I'll have to meet *him* or else he'll be around knocking on my door. Here's my key. Walk in like you owned the place. The night man's new since you were there. He won't know you." She stood up. "I may be a little long getting rid of *him*."

"That's all right, honey," he said. "Brush him off."

"I guess I'll have to," she said. She smiled at him. "A real son of a bitch, aren't you? Don't shoot me coming in the door, will you?"

"I will if you take too long getting there," he said.

"I won't be any longer than it takes," she said, and went out to Lexington Avenue.

The waiter came to the table. "Little lady didn't go away

mad, I trust? Didn't have no lovers' quarrel, now?" said the waiter.

"Not us," said Tommy. He paid the bill and took a taxi to Maida's hotel. The elevator boy was also new and minded his own business. Tommy undressed and got into bed, with the .38 under the covers beside his leg. There was a bridge lamp near the door, which he left burning, after fixing it so that it would throw most of its light on anyone who entered. He took a magazine from the bedside table and lit a cigarette. There was a radio on the lower shelf of the table, in case he wanted to turn it on. There were two bottles of rum and a bottle of rye and four bottles of Coca-Cola on the chiffonier, in case he got thirsty, and a Sterno stove, and a tin breadbox, which he had not investigated, and a bottle partly filled with cream on the window sill. He glanced around the room. "Aha, that we must get rid of," he said. He got out of bed and removed a man's glossy-print photograph from a leather frame. He put a match to it in two places and allowed it to burn on the tile floor of the bathroom.

"A man could stay here forever, if he had to," he told himself. He wished Carina didn't hold such grudges.

In the office things were quieting down. Over in the sports department the nightly bridge game already had been in session a good half hour. The men on the copy desk were either reading the nine-o'clock edition or just staring straight ahead, vacantly, fatigued. A few reporters were at their desks, writing letters or memos or maybe even belles-lettres, but not pieces for the paper. You could tell that. McGuire could tell it. After all these years there was little about the newspaper business he did not know, and one thing he knew was the look of a newspaper office at any given stage of getting out the paper. He leaned back, tilting his chair on its hind legs, gnawing at his empty pipe. Rather than appear to the guys on the copy desk the way they appeared to him, McGuire got up and wandered over to a window and studied the state capitol, this side of which he knew so well.

For eighteen years this side of the state capitol had been his horizon. Well, that was not precisely true. He had only been sitting at a desk facing the city room, and beyond it, this side of the capitol ten years—about ten years. There had been the times he had sat in on the night desk, when his horizon was the mail boxes and newspaper files. You could take those times out of the eighteen years. You could also take out the four months when he had undergone a miserable self-imposed exile as managing editor of the *Beacon*. The

Beacon being on Front Street, he hadn't even seen the capitol dome. At the *Beacon* his horizon had been Holzheimer's Storage Warehouse—Long Distance Moving. But anyway, to all intents and purposes he was now looking at what had been his horizon for either ten or eighteen years. Either way it was no good, and eighteen was only a little worse than ten. You didn't get used to hanging if you hung long enough. With some bitterness McGuire reflected that hoodlums could have painted dirty words on the other side of the state capitol, or a strange art commission could have painted it with pink and blue diagonal stripes, and he wouldn't have known about it. Oh, he'd have *heard* about it, and most likely in the case of a story as important as that he would have done the rewrite job on it. But in the ordinary course of his life, he would not have seen the words or the stripes. He didn't even see the other side of the capitol on his way to or from work, or going for a drink at Paddy's or the Elks'. When he bought shirts or pajamas or underwear, he bought them at Gross's, nowhere near the other side of the capitol. When he heard the call of the wild and went to Miss Elizabeth's, he went in the opposite direction from the capitol. All during the time he had been having the affair with Jess, he had had no occasion to study the other side of the capitol, since Jess's apartment, which she shared with another girl, was just up Hill Street from the office, a block and a half or two. It made him angry to have to face the fact that there probably were out-of-town lawyers and high-pressure guys who by actual count had seen the other side of the capitol many more times than he had, although he could have hit this side of the capitol with a silver dollar with a great deal more ease than Washington had pitched one across the Rappahannock and although he looked at the limestone pile (this side of it) five-sevenths of all the nights of his life.

Now, not suddenly but easily, he knew why he was quitting the paper this night.

Always there had been the *big* reason, but he didn't believe there was any one thing that had started him off in the direction of his decision. There had been, to be sure, his forty-third birthday in January last. But before that there had been the steadily increasing number of friends' names on the obit page. Not necessarily friends, but contemporaries in the sense that, in doing newspaper work, he had disregarded whatever difference there might have been between his age and the scoundrels' ages. People—persons—he *knew* well were dying and dying. Then there had been the gradual awareness that he was recording life (and, of course, death) but that he was passing it by. He was sitting it out as a night rewrite man on a not particularly outstanding newspaper. That undoubtedly was the big reason he had begun to think about quitting.

He looked over at Jess's desk. She was not there. Then he saw her coming out of a phone booth and going to Green's desk. She had some copy paper in her hand. She spoke to Green. Green nodded a few times and wrote something on a pad. He looked up at her and smiled, and McGuire could tell he was waving his hand, the sign he was giving his official "Good night." She went to her desk, took a towel and her purse out of the top drawer, and threaded her way among the desks to the ladies' room.

. . . Jess, for instance. Jess had been a reason, or perhaps a sub-reason, belonging under Passing Life By. He had been selfish with her, and after a while she had simply told him off. That was all there was to it. "It's time both of us were getting married," she had said. "Maybe not you to me or me to you, but from here on get another girl, or try Miss Elizabeth's." There was no special reason he shouldn't have married Jess. He had no wife anywhere, and the money angle didn't figure, because Jess could not have children and would have gone on working, and he still had the eight thousand dollars his mother had left him. It surprised him that Jess had felt so strongly about it then, strongly enough so that there was still no cordiality on her part. She called him Mac, but she would have no drinks with him, nor go to see Katharine Cornell with him, nor borrow cigarettes from him. He had had to get used to it, and for a long while he thought he had. Then there was the birthday, as well as Jess, with her coldness, and the realization that he was passing life by.

But then again, it was none of these things unless it was all of them. He wasn't quitting the paper because of Jess, or because he wrote about the life of the city and the state without participating in it, or because Senator Sam Fox had died yesterday of a heart attack in the Senate lunchroom in the state capitol. It was no more any one of these reasons than it was his newly discovered antagonism toward the capitol wall. Nor yet an unintelligent curiosity about the capitol's other wall. Still, the capitol's other wall was closer to being the reason. And then—this time suddenly and terrifyingly —he knew he was not going to quit, not tonight, not ever. He knew when he was well off. He knew when he had a good thing. He would stay with the paper and the paper would take care of him.

He turned his back on the state capitol and wandered back to his desk. Jess had returned to her desk and was putting on her hat and coat. On her way out she slowed down to wave at Green. He nodded and mumbled.

"Good night," said McGuire, as she went by his desk.

"Good night," said Jess. "Oh—good night," she said again, to something.

Like Old Times

I and this friend of mine we went in and sit down at the table
near ringside, *but not ringside*. It's as you go downstairs and
on the left as you get on the same level with the ringside it's
to your left, one table away from ringside. A good table.
Why it's a good table I happen to know because whereas the
big spenders, black marketeers, they always get ringside,
the ones that really count, *they* don't sit ringside. Ringside is
a sucker play. The real regulars practically never sit at ringside, becuss they know you get knocked your brains out by
the kids kicking you or giving you the elbow when they do
their chorus number if you're sitting ringside. Also you
spend. Sitting at ringside you get the feeling that everybody's looking at you and staring you in the back of the
head, so you get the bottle put on the table and there is
around twenty dollars right away. Right away. In spite of
possibly you may not drink up all that's in the bottle, still
once that bottle is put on the table—a double saw. Every
time, I tell you. It *works* that way. Put the bottle on the table
and by Christ if you get anything left out of twenty dollars
—Macy's window.

That's why what I noticed, I think ringside these people—
strangers? Out-of-town people? Here is this table. Ringside,
and I count the chairs. Five. Two couple and an extra man.
Five. I could be wrong, but isn't that the way you'd figure

it? Five? Two couple and one extra fellow along. That's the way I figured, and I was right. They got this table and the bottle, a bottle of Dewar's White Label, a bottle of club soda, a sort of bucket of ice, five setups. I think to myself, these people, who could they be? The ice is melting in the bucket. It's almost all water in the setups. A bunch of little flowers in the middle of the table. So on. Part of it adds up to big shots. The sauce there and the setups, but on the other hand, how important if they get this table ringside whereas I, Nobody from Noba Scotia, I sit at a good table. Ann-nonymous from Ann Arbor, I still get a better table. All right, I know Joe Lopez, but who doesn't know Joe Lopez, or who doesn't Joe Lopez know, more to the point. All you have to do is know Lopez and he'll give you a table if he has one, and if he doesn't have one he'll put one in for you. When I was a sheer nobody Lopez would give me a table just because I happened to know the fellow. Now he gives me a good table because if I happen to be in a hit show I get pointed out by the very same people that come and spend their moo in a room and want to see a person that's in a hit show. That's all. It isn't any more than that. If I happen to be in a hit show Joe recognizes that fact and lets me have a good table.

Well, so finally they come in, the ones at the ringside table for five. They come in five after twelve, and six after twelve whoever-it-is starts the floor show. No sooner are they on their duffs than they start the floor show. It's as if they were waiting for them, the ones at the table. I said big shots, because the way the booze was on the table, the flowers and setups, but it was more convincing the way the floor show starts when they sit down. That's a good way to tell it. These people, they weren't gunna be kept waiting.

Who *are* they? I ask myself. I look the hell at them. Don't recognize a soul. Not *one* of them. It's these four guys and a mouse. The mouse I must say is—I don't know who to compare her with. Yes. Yes, in a way I do. Paulette Goddard. That is, Paulette Goddard, except Goddard has no tragedy in her eyes. Goddard is never without a smile. Goddard, in other words, is smiling all the time. The dishes are there every minute of the time in Goddard's case. Like this. *See?* Every tooth in her head you can see. Big smile. Money in the bank. Option taken up. Big smile, with Goddard. No worries. No tragedy with Goddard. Whereas this mouse, as if they took turns giving her one in the puss, the four of them. Who the hell are they, say I.

Well, the most outstanding one is I should say around no less than three hundred pounds. A hunk of lard. Three hundred pounds if he's one ounce, but at the same time young-looking. That's one. Lard. The others, two of them don't deserve your consideration unless you take into consideration that the mouse, the Goddard type, I can't figure out who she's with. I said to my friend. You know my friend. It's Mary Beth. You know Mary Beth. "How do you figure that one?" I said. "Which one's she with?" "I don't know," says Mary Beth. "Not with the fat one, though," she says. "Why not?" I ask her. "Woman's instinct," she says. "Your cousin's carburetor," I said. "Then who *is* she with?" I asked her. "The one in the blue suit," she said. Well, he has his back to me and I can't very well see what he looks like. I see he's a big fellow, then he turns around and I guess he must be the one. He turns around to order something, glasses or soda or something. He's the one, all right. "How'd you know?" I asked Mary Beth. "Woman's instinct. He's the only one she isn't paying any attention to."

Right. I begin to take notice then. Goddard type, she isn't enjoying a minute of it, but she's spreading herself amongst all of them except Blue Suit. Equally. No more for one than the other. And the hell of it is, they look at her like she was trying to hustle them. She'll say something to one of them, probably something nice, making the effort, you know, and he'll look at her, look right down in the dress, listen to what she has to say, then by God—I watched it—by God all she gets for making the attempt is "Oh, yeah?" I guess this must of been going on all night. That's why she has this beat-up look when I first saw her.

Same thing with the others. The fat guy, or the other nonentity. She's as nice to them as it's possible to be. Everything but making a play. All she gets is this look. You know, like "Go 'way, you bother me." And meanwhile the blue-suit guy, he oughta punched them in the nose, but he's so busy talking and watching the floor show, he doesn't seem to notice. Never looks at her himself that I could see.

I dono, this goes on I dono how long. I didn't get as fascinated after a while so I didn't notice till then I happened to notice the two nonentity ones get up and go. They're gone, leaving the mouse and the fat one and the blue-suit charmer. Mary Beth is right. The mouse is with the blue-suit one. The others just powder out.

That gives me a chance to study the three of them. The mouse and the blue suit get up and sit where I can get a better look at them, one sitting on the one side of the fatso and the other on the other. Fatso by this time has sumpn to eat. A steak sandwich. But not like you and I have a steak sandwich. You and I have a steak sandwich and it's no sandwich. It's a piece of bread and a piece of steak and over to the one side another piece of bread. All right, that's what Fatso has, but Fatso puts the other piece of bread on top of the meat and eats it like a little hamburger. Picks it up, eats it like a hamburger, and boy you should have seen him devour it. He picks it up in his two hands and puts it in the one side of his mouth and he has these beady little eyes and by the expression on his face you'd of thought he was listening to himself eating it. That's exactly the way he looked, as if he was listening to it. I was fascinated. I never saw that before, a man taking a steak sandwich the size of that and pick it up in his fingers like a dainty little aw derve. Then I happened to look at the mouse, and she was fascinated too, but like she was gunna throw up. I thought she'd throw up. She sat there watching Fatso and like she was chewing. Yunk, yunk, yunk, her mouth'd go. In spite of herself. She didn't know she was doing it. And Fatso wiped his mouth with the back of his hand and then with the napkin and then wiped his hands with the napkin. I happened to notice his hands. The times I noticed a man's hands unless he happened to be shaking hands with me and trying to break my fingers it's very seldom. But Fatso must of originally been a very thin man. He had small hands and as if he had like a glove made of fat on. You could practically say that. As if he pulled the fat over small hands.

He sort of leaned over and said something to Blue Suit and Blue Suit called the waiter and without overhearing I could tell he was ordering another steak sandwich for Fatso. Right about then another couple came in. Newcomers. A little fellow looked like a doctor, and his wife. She had a mink coat cost her six thousand, Mary Beth said. I said to Mary Beth, "The leading abortionist of the Bushwick section," and she laughed. That's what he looked like, although he could of been a lawyer just as well. I don't know what he was, but I noticed Fatso didn't stand up for them although Blue Suit did. The mouse got up so Dr. Croveney could sit next to Fatso and the three guys started talking. The two women started talking and they might as well have been in another room for all the attention they got. When they wanted something they called the waiter themselves. Lit their own cigarettes. Ignored, is what I'm trying to say.

I was fascinated. Just then, or a couple minutes later, Chuck Robbins came in and he knows everything. "Sit down," I said to him. "Have a little smile." You know Chuck. "Gotta make a phone call but I'll be back," he said. "Sit down," I said, "I only want to ask you a question." "What's the question?" he said. "Who was the handball champion of Ireland in 1904?" I said. "Aw, go—" he started to say. "No, levelling," I said, "who's the stout party over there?" "Him?" said Chuck. "Why?" "I just wanted to know," I said. "Why?" said Chuck. "No reason," I said. "An operator," he said. "What makes you ask?" "Just been watching him," I said. Chuck nodded his head. "A lot of people are watching him." "Oh?" I said. "Why?" "That's it, they aren't sure why." "Like who?" I said. "The boys," he said. "You mean the law boys?" "Them too," said Chuck. "Why?" I said. "Now you're asking me *why*," said Chuck. "I don't know. He sells things. Is that enough for you?" "Not quite," I said. "What kinds of things?" Chuck looked at me. I known him a long time and he knows he can trust me. "Listen," he said, "the party is from Illinois. He sells things. And a lot of people are asking questions about him. In our set that should be enough for you."

It's getting like old times, isn't it?

Ellie

Although my sister and I were born in Texas, we have lived most of our lives in the North, from the time our father and mother were killed in a railroad accident, about twenty-five years ago. We were brought up by an aunt and uncle who lived in Westchester. I was eleven and Caroline was seven when Father and Mother died, and I never went back to Texas except briefly, on business. Our aunt and uncle sent me to camp in New Hampshire in the summer, and I went to boarding school when I was fourteen. Caroline, however, did go back to Texas several times and kept up a few friendships there. She was always lavishly entertained, and, naturally, when her Texan friends came to New York, she did her best to show them the town. This was simple enough; it usually involved one big evening of dinner at "21," the theatre, and supper at Larue's. Caroline lives her own life and I live mine, in apartments in different parts of town. Her job is in the midtown district, and I work downtown. For a sister and brother who are quite fond of each other, we are together infrequently, and it is unusual for her even to ask me in for a cocktail when she has some Texans to entertain.

When she telephoned me that Ham and Ellie Glendon were in town, I had to ask who they were. "He's a lawyer in Dallas, and they've never been to New York before," said

Caroline. "They're about my age, a year or two younger, but they were awfully nice to me the last two or three times I was down there."

"Uh-huh," I said, waiting.

"She's very pretty and quiet. He's—well—more Texan. He likes to get tight, and I thought—well—you know more places than I do. They'll want to go to '21,' but that won't be all. I mean he will . . . You're *not* being very helpful."

I laughed. "I get it. Colonel Glendon wants to raise a little hell. O.K. Does he carry a gun?"

"Probably," said Caroline. "They all do."

"Well, tell him to check the gun and I'll take you around. What did you have in mind?"

"Nothing in particular, but I just know he'll want to go someplace where I don't know the proprietor. Night-club kind of place. And it's my treat. You don't have to spend any money. I just want you to sort of steer us around. Black tie. My place at seven."

Ham Glendon was a rather large man with red hair and a red face, the kind that does not tan. In Caroline's hall, I saw one of those cream-colored hats with a half-inch band and I heard his voice, soft and for the moment not unpleasant but likely to become tiresome. He was wearing a double-breasted dinner coat and new patent-leather shoes and diamond-and-onyx studs. He called me Jim right off the bat, when he introduced me to his wife. She was something.

She was standing when I entered, Caroline having gone

to the kitchen. As I shook hands with her, I was surprised that I so quickly had to change my first impression of her height. She was not nearly as tall as I'd thought when I came into the room. She held her head back, but the top of it did not reach my chin. "I'm happy to know you," she said, and turned and sat down. Her figure was beautiful, and Neiman-Marcus had done their best by it—or probably had been delighted to clothe it, as much of it as was clothed. When she was turning to sit down, I caught her taking a quick look at me; she was trying to see what effect she had had on me, and when she found out, she dropped her eyes and reached for a cigarette.

We went to "21" and to "Oklahoma!," which Caroline and I had seen three times. At dinner, Ham and Caroline did most of the talking, about Texas friends whom I barely remembered or did not know. Ham would ask Ellie to fill in details on some of the people, and that was about all of her contribution to the conversation. I contributed even less, but I knew I wasn't bored and I was sure Ellie wasn't, because every once in a while she would look at me and smile. I remembered that Caroline had said she was quiet, and she didn't seem to expect much talk from me or to want to converse with me herself. In fact, she seemed to be quite happy just knowing that she had had an effect on me. At the restaurant and at the theatre other men looked at her too, and their admiration was something she breathed in.

When we came out of the theatre, Caroline suggested going back to "21" for a drink while we decided where we wanted to go. I wanted to go someplace where we could dance; there were some things I wanted to say to Ellie. But when we got to "21" Ham fixed that. "Jim, I raickon from here on we're in *your* hands." He laughed and I laughed.

"A pleasure," I said. "What kind of a place did you have in mind?"

"Well, more or less leave that up to you, Jim," said Ham.

"No, be frank, Ham," said Caroline. "My ne'er-do-well brother knows them all."

"Yes," I said.

"Well, *Harlem* is one place. We heard a lot about that Dorchester Ballroom."

"Oh, sure," I said, and thought of the way we were dressed. "You'll see some of the best dancing up there you'll ever see in your life. Of course, the smaller places don't begin to open up for quite a while, and if we wanted to go to one of them, I think we ought to change our clothes."

"Tell you the truth, Jim, we more or less had our hearts set on the Dorchester. You asked me to be *frank*."

"By all means," I said. I had the waiter bring a telephone to the table, and I called the manager of the Dorchester, a white man, whom I had known for many years. I was very careful to emphasize that I was with my *sister* and *some friends from Texas*. Max, my manager friend, was not obtuse and he promised he would save a box for us.

More than that, when we arrived at the Dorchester, he was waiting for us on the curb, and I was grateful, for there was a long queue of Negro boys and girls at the box office. Max took over and led us past the box office, and when we were inside, we were accompanied by Al Spode, the old-time Negro heavyweight who was head bouncer at the Dorchester, another old friend of mine.

They usually don't serve hard liquor at the Dorchester, but Max put a couple of coke bottles filled with bourbon on the table, and I thanked him and he went on about his business.

Ham turned out to like jazz and Caroline is a minor authority, so they were entertained by the two good bands. Our box, which was on the level of the dance floor and quite near the bandstand, was conveniently situated for me, or so I thought; the noise of the bands and the dancers would cover up the questions I was going to ask Ellie once we got settled. For the time being, we watched the superb dancing and drank our drinks. It was that way until one band finished a set. The dancers stood where they had stopped, waiting for the other band to start, and when it did, and the noise began again, I spoke to Ellie: "You know, if I'd had my way, we'd be where we could be dancing without being conspicuous, which we certainly are now." And she knew I meant the way we were dressed.

"Would we?" She half sneered and raised her eyes and let them indicate the dancers.

"Maybe Ham and Caroline will get bored soon and we can go someplace else. I don't think you're having too good a time."

"Oh, don't mind me."

"But I want you to have a good time. Do you like to dance? Because if you do, there are a few places where there's tea dancing. Now, for instance, if you were going to be free Saturday afternoon." I came down heavy on "free," so she would be sure I meant her, alone, without Ham.

"Saturday I was planning to have lunch with an old school friend I went to Randolph-Macon with." She paused and shifted in her seat. "But who ever heard of two girls just sitting around all afternoon in New York City? I imagine we'll have said all we have to say to each other by three, and after that I'll just saunter down Park Avenue in the direction of the Vanderbilt, and if I happened to meet somebody . . ."

"That's exactly the vicinity I was going to be in," I said. "Walking up Park Avenue around three."

I poured her a drink and one for myself, and I had that moment of peace when you know everything is settled and nothing much has been said. For all I know, Ham had been conversing in like manner with Caroline. Presently the set ended and the bands were changing again. The dancers slowed down, then stopped while the outgoing musicians left the bandstand and the incoming group took their places.

A boy and girl whom I had been half observing came over to the railing near our table. The girl leaned against the railing, her back toward us. The boy, who was very black, was facing in our direction. They had the confidence of artistry; they were surely the best dancers in the ballroom, and it may be that I myself showed applause by my facial expression. It doesn't much matter.

"Ham," said Ellie.

"Yes, honey," said Ham.

"Ham, that niggah's *lookin'* at me," said Ellie.

I looked at her and at her husband. "Now, wait a minute," I said.

"Which one, honey?" said Ham.

"Oh, God," said my sister, appealing to me.

I rose. "Up! Up, everybody! Come on!" I put a bill on the table and took Ellie's wrist. "We're getting out of here now, this minute."

"Not before I—" said Ham.

"Listen, you silly son of a bitch," I said. I pulled Ellie along with me, counting on Caroline to grab hold of Ham, which she did. We got out fast and stepped right into a taxi.

The ride downtown through the Park was a silent one until we were among the buildings south of Fifty-ninth Street. "Jim," said Ham, "you hadn't oughta called me a son of a bitch."

"I know," I said. "I'm sorry."

"Well, that's all right, then, if you apologize." He grinned. "Now wuddia say we all go over to the El Morocco club?"

"I don't think so," I said.

"*It's* all right, Jim," said Ham. "All's forgiven. I take into consideration you been living with Yankees too long."

"That may be," I said.

They dropped Caroline and then me. I went to bed with my mind made up that that was the last I'd ever see of Missy Ellie, but when Saturday came, I got out my car and at three o'clock I was cruising along lower Park Avenue, excited as a kid. But when I saw her, actually saw her, walking down Park, keeping her date with me, I grew old and cautious, and I drove away from her and trouble, her kind of trouble.

Life Among These Unforgettable Characters

The constant rediscovery by Americans of lovable, unforgettable American characters is a challenge to any American writer. Up to now this writer has done little or nothing about it, but this condition could not long endure. The following, therefore, is submitted as the author's attempt to participate in the movement, or trend. It is sloppily written chiefly because the author was unable to decide whether to do the piece as a magazine article, a revue sketch, or a script for a motion-picture short. Any resemblance to real persons, living or dead, is fortuitous. THE AUTHOR.

It was with sighs of relief that Mr. and Mrs. Mort pulled up to the filling station. They had been told upon leaving the town of X—— that the tank of their Lincoln Continental convertible would hold enough gas to get them to the town of Y—— but that it would be a good idea to make a stop at Arthur James Witherspoon's filling station, the only filling station between X—— and Y——. It was pointed out (unnecessarily, since Mr. and Mrs. Mort were experienced motorists) that when driving in the desert it is a wise thing now and then to halt, let some of the air out of your tires, stretch your legs, wash up, see to the gas and oil and water, and inquire as to the condition of the highway. Driving fatigue is thus lessened, and the motorcar itself is in better shape for continuing the journey. Unfortunately, upon leaving the town of X——, the Morts observed a sign that read, "90 MI TO ARTHUR JAMES WITHERSPOON'S," and then, ten miles farther, another sign that said the same thing.

Mr. Mort was doing the driving and he hoped his medium-young and attractive wife had not noticed the sign, but she had, all right. The third sign they saw reminded them that the next filling station was that of Arthur James Witherspoon, but gave no estimate of the distance. One thing the Morts knew: when they came upon a filling station it would be the only one, and it would be the one conducted by Arthur James Witherspoon.

The Morts kept an eye on the gas gauge and the speedometer, and had a fairly unpleasant time trying to recall what mileage they got on a gallon at what speed, and Mr. Mort, with his somewhat vague technical information, had the added worry about the effect of altitude on gasoline consumption. Unhappily, he could not recall whether you used more, or less, gasoline at high altitudes, and moreover he was not sure whether this particular desert was one of the high-altitude deserts or low ones.

The result was that he had chewed the inside of his cheek to the point where he was developing another salivary gland when, in the distance, about fifteen miles, he saw what could only be the filling station of Arthur James Witherspoon. He knew about mirages and suspected one, but when he turned to his wife she smiled; she, too, had seen the filling station, or what could only be the filling station. Praise God, they were right in their assumption.

When, some twelve or thirteen minutes later, they pulled up to the establishment of Arthur James Witherspoon, they at first saw no human being. But a moment after they stopped they saw an elderly man who had been half hidden by a rain barrel. He was sitting on a bench. Across his lap was an old .22 rifle, a Winchester octagonal-barrel pump gun. He wore a pair of levis and a blue shirt, both well bleached, a pair of white-and-brown saddle straps, and one of those cream-colored hats with half-inch bands that are affected by Westerners. The shoes were without laces. The man had what might be called a reluctant sunburn. His face and hands and arms were indeed sunburned, but not with the smoothness of the tan that indicates oils and lotions. He was sunburned because, in the desert, you just can't help it.

With the instinctive, well-mannered democracy that had got him into the Vine at Princeton, Mr. Mort called out to the elderly gentleman. "Howdy," he said.

"Hi ya," said the old gentleman.

"Fill 'er up," said Mr. Mort.

"Fill 'er up yourself," said the old gentleman.

Mr. Mort, as was his right, lightly punched his wife's thigh. "A character," he said, without moving his lips. Then, "Howdy," he repeated, starting to get out of the car. "Fill 'er up."

This time the old gentleman scratched himself and said, "*I* heard *you* the first time. Fill 'er up yourself."

"Oh," said Mr. Mort. He got out of the car and took the cap off the pipe leading to the tank of his car and unhooked the hose of the pump. He inserted the nozzle in the tank and then turned to Mr. Witherspoon. "Now what?" he asked.

"Just squeeze 'er, like a trigger. You seen it done a thousand times," said Mr. Witherspoon.

Mr. Mort smiled with almost boyish pleasure; he had

seen it done a thousand times, but he never had done it himself. It came easy to him, and the fuel began pouring in the tank. The fun of it partly took away from his chagrin at Mr. Witherspoon's reception.

Mr. Witherspoon now seemed unaware of the presence of his clients, and when Mrs. Mort got out of the car and said, "Where can I wash my hands, please?" Mr. Witherspoon said, "Don't do much washin' here. We're in the desert. You wanta gota the toilet . . ." and he half turned his head in the direction of the back of the filling station.

Mrs. Mort started in that direction, but before she had gone very far Mr. Witherspoon said, "Look out for rattlers."

Mrs. Mort froze. "What?"

"You better look out for snakes. I try to keep them off the place, but I can't be everywhere." With that he raised his rifle and aimed at a spot just inside the clearing. He fired, pumped, and fired again. Mr. and Mrs. Mort looked toward the spot at which he had aimed. A five-foot rattlesnake lay quivering and forever ineffectual. "Most likely be anothern along soon, unless she's in the toilet." To Mr. Mort he said, "Your wife wants to gota the toilet. Take that stick."

Mr. Mort, who had paused in the fuelling of his car, said, "She doesn't need any stick to—"

"She don't, but maybe the she-rattler's in there. I don't know. Suit yourself."

"Oh," said Mr. Mort. He replaced the pump hose and took the stick and preceded his wife to the rest room. While he was gone he heard another shot, and when he came back he said to Mr. Witherspoon, "Get the other one?"

"Nup," said Mr. Witherspoon.

"Missed her, eh?"

"Nup. Wasn't shootin' at anything."

"You weren't *shooting* at anything? I thought I heard you fire the gun."

"Rifle," said Mr. Witherspoon.

"I mean rifle. I was sure I heard you fire it, the rifle."

"You did, but that don't say I was shootin' at anything."

"Oh," said Mr. Mort, pretending to understand. "Guess I'll let some air out of the tires. Can I borrow a gauge?"

"In there in the creel, on my cot."

"Creel? Any fishing around here?" said Mr. Mort. He was speaking with the enthusiasm of a fisherman, but tolerantly incredulous as well.

"You look in that creel, you'll find a pair of dice, too, but I don't shoot crap with myself. You wanta borrow a gauge, it's in the creel."

Mr. Mort found the gauge and went about the business of letting some air out of the tires.

While her husband was thus engaged, Mrs. Mort reappeared and sauntered up to Mr. Witherspoon. "My, it must get awfully lonely here. Do you get to town often?"

"Evvy Christmas," said Mr. Witherspoon.

"What?"

"Never miss a Christmas in town. Nineteen year now. Wouldn't think of missing a Christmas in town."

"Oh, really? I imagine the radio must be a great consolation here. I see you have one."

"Wouldn't be without it," said Mr. Witherspoon. "Forty-eight, we'll send that Truman back to Missouri, where he belongs, him and the rest of 'em. Yes, sir, I listen to all them campaigns."

"Well, I hope you're right. My husband and I are Republicans, too."

"Y'are? Hmm. Well, I don't ask a person their politics or religion or where they come from. Uh-uh. There she comes." He raised his rifle, fired, and lowered it. "There she goes." A second rattlesnake bit the dust.

"Oh! Good shot!" said Mrs. Mort.

"The othern wasn't. Took two. Skins ain't worth as much when you got two bullet holes in 'em," said Mr. Witherspoon. He pulled out an old hunting-case watch, studied it, looked toward the sun, and nodded. "Watch is right," he said, and frowned. "Say, Ma'am, your husband's probly gonna want to clean the windshield. Why don't you do it for him while he's fooling around with them tires? Rag over there. Water in that bottle. Don't waste the water."

"Oh, let him do it. I'd just like to sit and talk for a few minutes."

"Too late now," said Mr. Witherspoon. "Thull be a truck along here now pretty soon and I don't like to have the place all cluttered up with cars and people, where I can't give the proper attention to evvabody. You just take that rag and wipe them bugs off the windshield and you'll be outa here that much sooner."

Mrs. Mort did as she was told, greatly to the surprise and delight of her husband, who regretted that he was unable to see the expression on her face as she removed the corpses of insects from the windshield. He asked Mr. Witherspoon how much he owed him.

Mr. Witherspoon squinted and stared at the pump. "Looks like two forty-eight from here."

"That's about it," said Mr. Mort.

"Two forty-eight. That's four ninety-six. Make it five dollars."

"Five dollars?" said Mr. Mort.

"Well, four ninety-six, then, if you object to paying the extra four cents."

"It's not the four cents I object to. It's the extra two forty-eight. What's that for?"

"Double. I charge everything double here. In the desert it's worth it. Put your two forty-eight in the tank, bub, and your car won't run very far on it. I got the gazzoline, so— well, what's the use explaining matters?"

"I see," said Mr. Mort. He took a ten-dollar bill from his wallet.

Mr. Witherspoon looked at it. "In the desk inside, top drawer, you'll find some fives and singles. Get your change there and put the ten in the second drawer with the twenties and fifties. Hate to hurry you, but I got another customer almost due about now."

"I wish you'd make the change yourself. I don't like to handle somebody else's money."

"Why, I trust you, bub. Anyhow, you can't get very far on the desert. Only one road, bub, next town fifty-five mile from here."

"I see," said Mr. Mort. He did as instructed and then

joined his wife in the car. Mr. Mort was now disagreeable. He started the motor, and as he was pulling away he heard the voice of Mr. Witherspoon.

"Hurry back," said Mr. Witherspoon, and looked again at his watch.

The wardroom was quiet, next to the quietest it ever got. Radio Tokio was playing the Fred Astaire record of "Beginner's Luck." A Torpecker pilot was playing acey-deucey with the skipper of the Torpecker squadron, and about the only sound they made was when they would put a new man on the board, snapping it very deliberately on the hardwood. From the wardroom mess next door could be heard the murmurs of a bridge game—four fighter pilots who had been playing among themselves, the same four, since the carrier had left Pearl Harbor. One of the officers from Damage Control was reading *The Autobiography of Lincoln Steffens* and he had gas on his stomach. A Negro steward was pushing a long-handled dust brush across the deck, bumping the legs of the heavy chairs, which he obviously had no intention of moving. At infrequent intervals some unimportant announcement would come over the squawk box: "Now, hea' this . . ." Most officers had either hit the sack or were in their rooms writing letters. It had been a good day; three deckloads had taken off and all had returned, mission accomplished. There was the usual after-supper rumor that a Betty had turned up on the radar screen, but this rumor had first made its appearance the night after the ship had left Eniwetok, and that was many, many days ago, and even if a Betty did turn up, that was another, and smaller, carrier's problem. That is to say, it was up to another carrier to take care of the Betty; it was, of course, this carrier's problem if the Betty *hit* this carrier.

Delaney, the middle-aged correspondent, came in the wardroom and searched the bookcase for a book he had been reading. The Damage Control officer made a rude noise and Delaney saw that the officer had the book, and Delaney went over to one of the davenports and sat down with Forrest, a fighter pilot. Delaney nodded and said hello, and Forrest took his cigar out of his mouth. "Hi, Mr. Delaney," he said. "Getting enough to write?"

"Oh, yes. Not so easy to get it back, though."

"I guess that is tough. How *do* you get it back?" Forrest was a friendly kid. He offered Delaney a cigar, which Delaney declined.

"Like regular mail. When a can comes alongside, we put our stuff in a special pouch, but it has to be censored at Pearl. If you write a letter, it gets to wherever you write it before our stuff gets to New York."

"You'd think they'd make some arrangements about that."

"They're always talking about it," said Delaney. "You want to play some gin?"

"Thank you, sir, but I never learned it. Only games I play are acey-deucey and, of course, poker. There's a poker game in the ready room if you'd like to play that. I didn't feel like it tonight, so I just came down here to commune with nature."

Delaney laughed. "They don't like transients in the poker game."

"Sometimes they do, if the transients are steady losers."

"Oh, sure, in that case," said Delaney.

"Sure you won't have a cigar, sir?"

"Yes, I think I'll change my mind. How about a cup of coffee? I'll get it."

"Oh, no. I'll get it."

"No, I was going to anyway. You sit still." Delaney went to the wardroom mess and brought back two cups of coffee and two pieces of rhubarb pie.

"Say, thanks. Not bad, not bad."

They ate the pie and drank the coffee in silence, and when they had finished, Delaney said, "Now I'll have that cigar you threatened me with."

"Sorry, I forgot. Here." Forrest handed Delaney the cigar, a brand that would have cost sixty cents straight at home.

"Good cigar," said Delaney.

"I guess so. I never smoked cigars before I joined the Navy. A lot of things I never did before I joined the Navy. A lot of things I do in the Navy I won't do when I get out."

"I'll bet," said Delaney.

"That's something I always wanted to ask somebody, Mr. Delaney. You were in the last war. Just how tough is it, getting readjusted and all that, when you go back to civil life?"

Delaney hesitated. "I don't think I'm the right one to ask that question, Forrest. I wasn't in the real Army. I was in a thing called the S.A.T.C."

"S.A.T.C.?"

"Students' Army Training Corps. Also known as the Saturday Afternoon Tea Club. One day I was just an ordinary student in college, the next day I was technically in the Army, getting paid, wearing a uniform. Then again, one day I was wearing a uniform, technically in the Army—next day, a student. Living on the same campus all the time. Not much of a reconversion problem there, so I don't know. You worried about it? I guess everybody is."

"Not worried, exactly. But I think about it. I wonder about it."

"Most of the fellows I knew that saw action in the last one—practically none of them would talk about it for two or three years. Quite a few of them were sore at guys that weren't in it."

"About the same now, I guess," said Forrest. He appeared to be looking into the far distance. "I'll be better off than most of these jokers. Most of them don't know a thing but how to fly an airplane. I'm better off because I have a year of law school behind me. My old gent was a lawyer. Still is."

"You going to practice law?"

"I sure am. I have the spot all picked out—not with my old gent. It's a place where we go for the summer, in New England. It's the county seat. I have it all planned. I'll finish law school—first get married and *then* finish law school. Then I'm going to build a house. Not a summer house. I'm going to build one right in the town. Probably brick. I'll leave most of that to my wife, because she'll be the one that spends most of her time there. But I'm going to build my office to suit myself. It won't be on the main drag, but right around the corner from the courthouse. One story, see? Two rooms. One sort of outer office, reception-room kind of thing, behind a fence. I always liked those fences— you know, those fences they have in small-town lawyers' offices. Desks, chairs, tables, my diploma hanging on the wall, filing cases. All that will be in the outer office, where the public can see it. Very respectable, very official-looking. But my own office—the inner sanctum, so to speak—that's going to be completely unconventional. I'm going to have a head and a tub and a phone extension in there. And a radio. In my office I'm going to have all the junk I've collected all my life. For instance, when I was fifteen, I shot a deer. Deer head's going to be in there. Cups and stuff I won playing tennis. Pictures. All my favorite pictures. Reproductions of Grant Wood and van Gogh and some my girl painted at a place where she goes on Lake Michigan.

"Let's see what else. Oh, Christ, this is going to be the god-damnedest lawyer's office you ever saw, but anybody that doesn't like it can get another boy. I'll have a television set by that time. In my office. All the books I like. Oh, and a bar. A special closet that I'll keep my liquor in, with a Frigidaire and glasses and some ale tankards that my old man bought in England, but I can wangle them out of him. I think I may put them on a shelf on the wall of my office."

"You didn't say 'bulkhead,' " said Delaney.

"Intentionally," said Forrest. "Not that I'm going to forget all about the Navy. For instance, I imagine I'll join the

Coast Guard Reserve, or whatever they call themselves. I'm going to have two boats. One about a thirty-three-footer that'll sleep four comfortably. There'll be a lot of those, good ones, after this little caper is over. Cheap, too, I'll bet. The other, I haven't made up my mind. My wife likes to sail She's had boats all her life. I call her my wife, but you know what I mean. My future wife. A *very* elegant woman, absolutely four-O, as the Trade School boys say. Well, she can pick her own boat. I haven't made up my mind about a car. They'll be bringing out some wonderful stuff when this thing is over, so I'm not even planning about a car. I *would* like to have a motorcycle. We can get along with one car and the motorcycle, because I won't need the car much, having my office right around the corner from the courthouse, so my wife can use the car most of the time. You know McNamara, in our squadron? He comes from a little town about forty miles from this place, so I imagine we'll be seeing a lot of Mac and his wife."

"What about a plane?"

"Oh, the hell with that. Not right away, anyway." Forrest paused to relight his cigar, and as Delaney waited for him to go on, the squawk box became alive for that second before any message comes over. Then it came; they only needed to hear two notes on the bugle and they were on their feet. The acey-deucey game stopped; the Damage Control officer dropped his book; the bridge players' chairs scraped the deck.

"Taw-pedo defense, taw-pedo defense. Awl han's man yaw battle stations. Taw-pedo defense."

Forrest and Delaney looked at each other as they began to jog-trot. Forrest smiled. "You come and visit us, sir," he said, and smiled again. Then he began to run, and Delaney wearily trotted after him.

Clara

Dixon checked in at the hotel a little before six o'clock. He went to his room and washed and then sat in the lobby to wait for Muldoon, the lawyer, with whom he was dining. Officially it had been spring for several weeks, but there was a nip in the air and there was a fire going in the great fireplace. The people in the lobby were mostly men—salesmen, very likely, since Dixon did not recognize any of them as either natives of the village or summer people. Some of them went into the dining room together and some to the bar, singly and in pairs. As always when he came to the village out of season, Dixon was mildly surprised that life went on in the absence of the summer people. They had their own life, the natives, and in a curious way the fact called for respect. It was evidence of independence, if you cared to put it that way, and Dixon admired independence, good or bad, for its own sake. He was on his second cigarette and thinking of going to the bar when Muldoon appeared. Dixon rose to greet him, smiling and waiting for Muldoon to speak first, for the truth was Dixon momentarily forgot whether he and Muldoon were on a first-name or a last-name basis.

"Good evening, Charles," said Muldoon.

"Bill, nice to see you," said Dixon.

"Sorry it had to be under these circumstances," said Muldoon.

"Yes," said Dixon. "Thank you for your letter. We all appreciated it. Mother always thought very highly of you."

"No more than I of her. That was a fine woman—Mrs. Dixon. A fine woman. Her kind don't grow on trees."

"That's right," said Dixon. It most certainly was right; at least no mother he ever knew had grown on a tree. Muldoon apparently was thinking the same thing.

"I mean—well, all too rare these days," said Muldoon. "Will we go in and put on the feed bag? I'll just put my hat and coat here. I guess there won't be much trouble finding a place to sit, not like it was last summer." He hung up his hat and coat, there being no hat-check girl, and they went to a table against the wall. The headwaitress, a stout, pretty woman, came to take their order.

"Good evening, Mr. Muldoon," she said. "Mr. Dixon."

"Hello, Clara," said Muldoon.

"Hello, Clara," said Dixon. "You here?" He shook hands with her, an unexpected ceremony involving some awkwardness on her part in transferring pencil and order blank to her left hand, in which she held the menu.

"Sorry to hear about your mother, Mr. Dixon," she said.

"Thanks, Clara."

"Wonderful woman. We all admired her greatly."

"Thank you," said Dixon. His mother had been dead more than two months, and in town he had got used to the fact.

"The roast beef is nice tonight. Not for *you*, Mr. Muldoon"—she smiled—"but Mr. Dixon might like it."

"You on a diet, Bill?"

"Friday," said Muldoon.

"Oh, that's right. Well, if you can stand seeing me eat it, I think I'll have it."

"Rare," said Clara, writing it down. "Mr. Muldoon, how about the lobster Newburg?"

"Oh, Clara, you oughta know better than that."

"Oh, come on now, Mr. Muldoon," said Clara.

"Anyway, I had it for lunch," said Muldoon. He and Clara laughed heartily and Dixon did the best he could. "Give me some of that fish chowder and the fried oysters."

"Would you like something from the bar? Cocktails, or beer?"

"I'd like a Martini," said Dixon.

"Dry," said Clara.

"Yeah, I'll have one, too," said Muldoon.

"Two Martini cocktails, dry. Uh-huh. Coffee with the meal or after?"

"No coffee for me," said Muldoon.

"Later for me," said Dixon.

"All righty, thank you," said Clara, leaving.

Muldoon began to nod. "Clara's—well, Clara's all right again."

"Why do you say 'again'?" said Dixon.

"You knew Dan," said Muldoon.

"Sure. All my life. Why?"

"Out after rabbit last fall. Gun went off. Just about took his leg off. Dragged himself over a half a mile to the road. Picked up. Dead. Trail of blood where he dragged himself, over a half a mile."

"Good Lord, I didn't know that. How could a thing like that happen to Dan? One of the best man handling guns I ever knew. In fact, he taught me everything I know about them, rifle and shotgun."

"Mm-hmm. That's what *everybody* said. They do a hell of a lot of talking in a place this size, if you know what I mean."

"I *think* I do."

"Why would Dan Larkin want to kill himself? And if he *did* want to kill himself, why shoot himself in the leg?"

"And drag himself all that distance to the road?" added Dixon.

"Well, some of the backbiters said he didn't want to make it look like suicide. The insurance. In a minute." Muldoon stopped talking while a waitress served the cocktails. He spoke again when she went away. "Clara wouldn't have collected if it'd been suicide, and Dan wasn't in any too good shape financially."

"Hell, I wish I'd known that," said Dixon.

"Don't give it another thought. Dan didn't commit any suicide."

"Of course not," said Dixon.

"There wasn't much insurance anyway. You see for yourself, Clara had to take a job. Pretty hard on Clara, you know, taking what you might call a public job like this headwaitress one, even with knowing what some people were saying. Not all, of course, but some. Enough." Muldoon twirled his glass. "Well, too bad you had to come down when

I'm batching it. Mrs. Muldoon would have got together a nice, home-cooked meal."

"Tell her I'm sorry I missed her."

"I'll do that," said Muldoon. "Did you bring all the papers with you?"

"Yes, I have some in my pocket and some in my room upstairs," said Dixon. "I have the more important ones here, if you'd like to have a look at them."

"Yes, I can go over them now while we're eating. I have to go to the Stations at ha' past seven. Stations of the Cross. Every Friday during Lent. But I can take a look at these now and see you later or you can come in my office in the morning. That'd be better, I guess. You get a good night's sleep and come in in the morning." They discussed the business of Dixon's mother's estate until it was time for Muldoon to leave, and then Dixon went out and sat in the lobby to smoke a cigar.

He took a chair from which he could observe the dwindling activity in the dining room. At nine o'clock, Clara appeared at the double glass doors and closed them and hung up a sign which read, "Breakfast 7-9; Lunch 12-1:30; Dinner 6-8:30." She did not see him. He rose and went to the dining-room entrance, and now she saw him. He held up a hand to signal to her, and she opened one of the doors.

"Well, Charlie, didn't you get enough to eat?" she said, smiling.

"I have my car outside. I'll give you a ride home," he said.

"Oh, that's all right. It isn't much of a walk."

"Or better yet, I'll buy you a drink."

"Where? Here?"

"Sure. Anywhere you say," he said.

"I'm one of the hired help here, you know. I don't often go in the bar when I'm not working. . . . All right. Wait'll I change my dress. I'll meet you inside."

The bar was a dark, low-ceilinged room, with simulated flagstone flooring and antiqued panelling and booths. Dixon waited in one of these, the booth farthest from the door.

"I wasn't long, was I?" said Clara. She was wearing a smart black suit, a white shirtwaist, and a small black hat trimmed in white. She sat across the table from him.

"Not a bit too long, not a bit too soon."

"My Lord, it must be twenty years since you said that to me. It *is* twenty, if not more. You're what? Forty-three."

"Four."

"That's right." She looked up at the waiter. "Hello, Norm. Give me a rye and ginger ale."

"Mr. Dixon?"

"Give us *two* rye and ginger ales and two Scotch and sodas, if you have Scotch."

"Blend. Scotch type."

"O.K. Two ryes, two Scotch types. Save yourself a trip."

Clara took a cigarette and Dixon was pleased, as he had been earlier, at the seemingly unchanged beauty of her skin, white as her teeth. She leaned back in her corner and smiled at him. "I guess Bill Muldoon brought you up to date on me."

"He told me about Dan. I didn't know it before."

"I know you didn't, Charlie. I'd have heard from you if you knew."

"That's right. I'm glad you know that," said Dixon.

"You were always one of our favorite people. It didn't make much difference if we never saw you much. Why should we? We had our life and you had your life. How's your wife? Jean, isn't it?"

"Yes. She's fine."

"Let's see, you have two sons and a daughter. I have two daughters. My eldest is the same age as your second boy. Sixteen. You should *see* her, Charlie. She's a beauty. The younger one's going through that ungraceful stage now, but she'll be all right, too."

"I'd like to see them."

"They're both at the high-school auditorium tonight, rehearsing the show. Clara has the lead, she's the eldest. Mind you, rehearsing now, *already*, and the play won't be put on till commencement. Clara graduates this year."

"Is she going to college? . . . Thanks, Norm."

"Not till the year after next, if then. Right now I can't afford it and I don't want her to go away so young, sixteen, so she's going to take the secretarial course at high next year."

"That sounds like a good idea, as long as it doesn't keep her back."

"Oh, she's bright, too. Sixteen, you know, and graduating from high. I was almost nineteen, but of course I was dumb and flighty. They wouldn't have graduated me if it hadn't been for Poppa being on the school board. Is your eldest in college?"

"Uh-huh. Yale—or was last week."

"Like his father, I guess. A real hell-raiser. Will you ever forget that car? The yellow one. Mormon?"

"Marmon."

"No wonder I thought of Mormon, all the girls that— well, why bring *that* up?" She fell silent for a moment. "It's nice to be sitting here and having a drink with you and talking over old times." She looked at him and her mouth opened, and she looked away and then back at him. "Well, *say* something," she said presently, pretending to be irritated.

"It goes without saying," he said.

"Uh-huh," she said. She took a cigarette from the pack on the table. He held a match for her, but she shook her head. "I'd rather do it myself. And I notice your hand's shaking, too."

"Sure it is. Why not?"

"I thought I was the only one," she said. She exhaled smoke from deep inside her. "Just think, I could have married you one summer."

"You sure could have."

"And how long would *that* have lasted? All the way to September. But I *wanted* to. I mean, if it was only you, I would have. But not the whole Dixon family, and going to New York every winter. It's a good thing for the two of us I had a grain of sense. I was better off with Dan."

"Did you ever say anything to Dan about us?"

"Dan? When Dan and I got engaged, we made an agreement. If I didn't ask *him* about the *girls* from the summer people, he wouldn't ask *me* about the *boys* from the summer people. Fair exchange is no robbery. Poor Dan! I suppose Bill Muldoon told you the talk that went around that he committed suicide."

"Yes, he did. *I* didn't believe it."

"There wasn't a son of a bitch in the world that could make Dan commit suicide, and that includes me, although I'm not a son of a bitch."

"Far from it," said Dixon.

"Are you starting early tomorrow? Back to New York, I mean."

"Not till after lunch."

"Then, in that case, will you part with some of the Dixon millions and buy me another rye and ginger? I relax with you, Charlie."

"We can have doubles," said Dixon.

"Doubles, and maybe you won't go back tomorrow afternoon, either," she said. "Tell me honestly, do you think I've put on too much weight?"

"I like what I see," he said.

She raised her eyebrows. "That isn't a Marmon you have out there?" She mumbled the words.

"What?"

"What do you like about me, Charlie?"

"You'd laugh if I told you."

"No, I wouldn't. No, I wouldn't. . . . Oh, hello, Norm."

"Two double ryes and two double Scotch types, please," said Dixon.

"Sit over here," said Clara, when the waiter had gone. He sat beside her, and when he kissed her, she took a deep breath. "Now go back on your own side of the fence and tell me what you like about me."

"You'll laugh."

"I *won't* laugh."

"All right. Your independence."

"Oh, the hell with *that*," she said.

Secret Meeting

Eben Townsend was sitting on the screened-in porch smoking his after-dinner cigar when he heard the telephone ring. His wife answered it. She called to him, "For you. Joe Travers."

"Oh, hell," said Eben as he went to the phone. "What does *he* want?" He knew what Joe Travers wanted.

"Eben? . . . Joe. Not coming to the meeting?" Travers' voice was brisk.

"What meeting was that, Joe?"

"Board meeting about Doc Bushmill and you-know. Everybody here but you, Eben." Travers waited.

"Oh, yes, that's right. I'll put on a coat and be right over."

"We won't start till you get here," said Travers.

"Won't be five minutes," said Eben, and hung up. "Special School Board meeting. I forgot about it," he explained to his wife.

"*Forgot* about it. Hmph," said his wife. "I'll bet a dollar it's the secret meeting and you're trying to duck it. The one about—"

"If it's secret, *keep* it secret," said Eben. He went upstairs and changed from his bedroom slippers to shoes and put on a necktie and a tropical worsted coat. He got his straw hat from the porch table and started the short walk to the high-school building, where the Board had its meeting room.

The parked station wagons and convertibles near the movie house were more numerous than usual for so early in the season, and a lot of summer people were taking in the first show, which went on around seven. In the block ahead, a group of boys and girls—high-school students—whom Eben knew were standing in front of the drugstore, and Eben changed his course to avoid passing them. They couldn't possibly know that this was the night for the meeting, although they all surely knew a meeting was soon to be held. He turned the next corner and went down the back street to the high-school building.

As soon as he saw the building, he almost lost his temper; it looked as though half of the entire first floor was lit up. That was certainly a beautiful way to conduct a secret meeting. Someone must have turned on the lights on his way to the Board meeting room in the rear of the building and left them on. Eben went to the back door. It was open, as was the door of the meeting room.

The six other members of the Board were sitting around one end of the long conference table, the too-long conference table. The room was used for faculty meetings, but the table was still too long—an extravagance that Eben, as cashier of the bank, had been the first to point out. The other members exchanged hellos with Eben, and Joe Travers immediately took charge, by nodding to those on one side of the table and nodding to those on the other side, clearing his throat, and placing the tips of his fingers on the table.

"Just a minute, Joe," said Eben. "If this was supposed to

be a secret meeting, I don't see why you had to advertise it, lighting up the entire building."

"You're right, Eben, but the harm's done, so we'll leave 'em on. May be a good thing after all. Cammyflodge. A lot of people most likely expect this meeting to take place in one of our private houses, if you see what I mean. Having it here with the place all lit up, a lot of people won't expect that. However . . ." He moved his mouth as though chewing something, and after the pause he began again. "There would have been a good reason to hold this particular meeting in a private house instead of school property. This is an unofficial meeting, and having it here may give it sort of the aspect of official. It is nothing of the kind. Notice I am not calling the meeting to order. Notice we are not going to have any minutes or any other regular proceedings. My gavel's in the drawer, and that's where it'll stay. In fact, I ain't even going to stand up. What I'll do, I'll try to get the discussion started, and we won't have anybody presiding. We'll keep it informal and unofficial."

"Well, let's get it started and let's get it over with," said Eben.

"Suits me right down to the ground," said Joe. "Luckily, our only lady member is a married woman and, the fact is, a grandmother, so we can speak more freely than otherwise. Mizz Drayton, Lucy, you came prepared for a frank discussion, I hope."

Lucy Drayton nodded. She was prepared, but reluctant— Eben could see that.

"We have a very nasty situation," said Joe. "I'm not going to mention any names, but I think we all know the situation. The situation is where a member of our faculty is accused of two crimes, or at least offenses. One, on Commencement Night, getting publicly intoxicated. Two, of forcing his attentions on a young female student while intoxicated and on school property. These offenses took place at the end of the school term, a little over two weeks ago, and we're not supposed to have a regular official meeting till August, but all of us received a number of anonymous letters calling our attention to the—uh—actions of this member of our faculty, and whereas anonymous letters should usually be thrown in the wastebasket, not when it's a matter of the morals of the children in our public schools. Here you have a particular kind of a situation.

"Now then. I called this informal, unofficial get-together to find out what we ought to do about the situation. Whether we ought to have a special official meeting or just go on ignoring the situation till it's called to our attention officially. Personally, what I would do with a drunken bum that goes around molesting our high-school girls, I would hand him his hat and give him a good, swift kick and see to it he never gets another job in the public-school system in the whole United States."

Joe Travers finished, and there was a long silence. The other members kept looking at Joe and he looked at each one individually, but no one accepted the implied invitation to take up where he had left off. Finally, Joe said, "Eben what about you? I started the discussion, and we're not getting anywhere just sitting here cooped up on a pleasant summer's evening."

"Amen to that," said Eben. "Only thing I was wondering, where do we expect to get? There weren't any charges filed against the member of the faculty."

"You said yourself, Joe, anonymous letters . . ." said Mrs. Drayton.

"What do we know? What facts have we got?" said Sam Locke, the oldest member. "Oh, I *heard* things about the—gentleman being intoxicated. The rest of it, nobody said anything to me about it except the anonymous letters, which I threw away."

"Now, wait a minute," said Joe. "I'm as much against anonymous letters as anybody, only when it comes to—well, where there's smoke, there's fire."

Ed Wales, the druggist, spoke up: "It's understood this talk is all unofficial—right? Well, unofficially, I saw the party in question Commencement Night. After all the exercises were over. And unofficially I'd say he had a few too many. I took the night off, of course, but I went back to the store just when Frank, my new assistant, was locking up, and when we got through locking up, the party in question was standing out in front of my store. He was heeling and toeing, feeling pretty good, humming to himself. I said good night and he said good night, and I went home. But he wasn't *with* anybody, girl or man. I'd think if he had a . . ." He stopped and glanced embarrassedly at Mrs. Drayton.

"Go on, Ed," she said.

"Well, I don't know," said Ed.

"I know what you're thinking," said Joe. "You're think-ing if he'd been molesting girls, he wouldn't be alone when you saw him. That don't follow."

"The letter I got—I only got one—" said John Eltring-ham, the Chevrolet dealer, "the funny business was sup-posed to be in a car parked somewheres near here. Well, sir, there wasn't a hell of a lot of chance—pardon me, Lucy—but there wasn't much chance for any funny business with both cops riding around seeing nothing was stolen out of the cars. Another thing I'd like to know, not because this faculty member bought a car from me, but why didn't the girl let out a yell? You could hear a good yell from one end of the vil-lage to the other. I know you could when I was a young fel-low."

"Maybe nowadays the young girls don't yell," said Sam Locke. Everybody laughed but Joe Travers.

"That's right," said Eben. "They save their yelling till they have a couple of days to think it over."

"And then write anonymous letters," said Ed Wales.

"Yeah," said John Eltringham, "or else maybe she didn't yell because she thought it was somebody else."

"There's a lady present," said Joe.

"That's all right," said Mrs. Drayton. "John may be right. Why *didn't* she yell?"

"Well, I didn't think *you'd* make a joke out of it," said Joe.

"I'm not, Joe, but if she had yelled, the policemen would surely have heard her," said Mrs. Drayton. "Or somebody. And the faculty member was on the stage with us, right down in the auditorium, till the exercises were over, and then Ed saw him a little later in front of his drugstore. Mind you, I don't favor letting our faculty make overtures to the girls, but I don't know . . ."

After a long and thorough clearing of his throat, Morton Atherton, the watchmaker, spoke up: "*I* brought *my* letter with me. I bet I'm the only one."

"No, I did, too, Morton," said Joe.

"Well, let's see if yours checks with mine. I'll read it. 'Dear Sir: How much longer are you going to permit a member of the faculty to remain there if he becomes intoxicated and is a menace to the girl students by attempting to prey upon them as in an automobile on Commencement Night? He is also a disgrace to the faculty and is very inefficient as a teacher. Signed: Disgusted Taxpayer.' Yours check, Joe?"

"Yes. Word for word," said Joe.

Eben placed a hand on Mrs. Drayton's shoulder. "Now, don't you take offense at this, Lucy, but that letter sounds like a female to me."

"I think you're right," said Mrs. Drayton.

"Another hunch I have, if we want to go into this seriously, we could ask for the records and find out who he flunked among the girls. Or shall we just forget about it? How about a vote? Joe?"

Joe looked around and knew what the vote would be. "No, no vote. This is informal, unofficial."

Sam Locke stood up. "In that case, I informally and unofficially move we informally and unofficially go home. These chairs are hard sitting." The others rose.

"Right," said Ed Wales.

"Mm-hmm," said Morton Atherton.

"All the goddam foolish wastes of time," said John Eltringham.

"Well, there might of been something in it," said Joe Travers.

"Uh-huh," said Eben. "Lucy, just to be on the safe side, I think I better walk you home."

"A pleasure," said Mrs. Drayton.

Drawing Room B

Nobody big had taken Leda Pentleigh to the train, and the young man from the publicity department who had taken her was not authorized to hire the Rolls or Packard that used to be provided for her New York visits. Nor had they taken their brief ride from the Waldorf to Grand Central. This time, she was riding west on the Broadway and not the Century, had come to the station in an ordinary taxicab, from a good but unspectacular hotel north of Sixtieth Street. Mr. Egan, it is true, was dead, but his successor at Penn Station, if any, did not personally escort Leda to the train. She just went along with the pleasant young hundred-and-fifty-a-week man from the publicity department, her eyes cast down in the manner which, after eighteen years, was second nature to her in railroad stations and hotel lobbies, at tennis matches and football games. Nobody stopped her for her autograph, or to swipe the corsage which the publicity young man's boss had sent instead of attending her himself. Pounding her Delman heels on the Penn Station floor, she recalled a remark which she was almost sure she had originated, something about the autograph hounds not bothering her: it was when they didn't bother you that they bothered you. Of course, it was Will Rogers or John Boles or Bill Powell or somebody who first uttered the thought, but Leda preferred her way of putting it. The thought, after all, had been thought by thousands of people, but she noticed it was the way *she* expressed it that was popular among the recent johnny-come-latelies when they were interviewed by the fan magazines. Well, whoever had said it first could have it; she wouldn't quarrel over it. At the moment of marching across Penn Station, there seemed to be mighty few travellers who would take sides for or against her in a controversy over the origin of one of her routine wisecracks; far from saying, "There goes Leda Pentleigh, who first said . . ." the travellers were not even saying, "There goes Leda Pentleigh— period." The few times she permitted her gaze to rise to the height of her fellow-man were unsatisfactory; one of the older porters raised his hat and smiled and bowed; two or three nice-appearing men recognized her—but they probably were Philadelphians in their thirties or forties, who would go home and tell their wives that they had seen Leda Pentleigh in Penn Station, and their wives would say, "Oh, yes. I remember her," or "Oh, yes. She was in Katie Hepburn's picture. She played the society bitch, and I'll bet she's qualified." Katie Hepburn, indeed! It wasn't as if Katie Hepburn hadn't been in pictures fifteen years. But no use getting sore at Katie Hepburn because Katie was a few years younger and still a star. At this thought, Leda permitted herself a glance at a Philadelphia-type man, a man who had that look of just about getting into or out of riding togs, as Leda called them. He frowned a little, then raised his hat, and because he was so obviously baffled, she gave him almost the complete Pentleigh smile. Even then he was baffled, had not the faintest idea who she was. A real huntin'-shootin' dope, and she knew what he was thinking—that here was a woman either from Philadelphia or going to Philadelphia and therefore someone he must know. The gate was opened, and Leda and Publicity went down to her car. Publicity saw that she was, as he said, all squared away, and she thanked him and he left, assuring her that "somebody" from the Chicago office would meet her at Chicago, in case she needed anything. Her car was one of the through cars, which meant she did not have to change trains at Chicago, but just in case she needed anything. (Like what, she said to herself. Like getting up at seven-thirty in the morning to be ready to pose for photographs in the station? Oh, yes? And let every son of a bitch in the Pump Room know that Leda Pentleigh no longer rated the star treatment?)

In her drawing room, Leda decided to leave the door open. There might, after all, be a Coast friend on the train. If she wanted to play gin with him—or her—she could do it, or if she wanted to give her—or him—the brush, she knew how to do that, too. Her window was on the wrong side of the car to watch people on the platform, and she sat in a corner where she could get a good look at the passengers going by her door. She opened a high-class book and watched the public (no longer so completely hers) going by. They all had that beaten look of people trying to find their space; bent over—surely not from the weight of their jewelry boxes and briefcases—and then peering up at the initial on her drawing room, although they could plainly see that the room was occupied by a striking, stunning, chic, glamorous, sophisticated woman, who had spent most of the past week in New York City, wishing she were dead.

She drove that little thought out of her mind. It would do no good now to dwell on that visit, ending now as the train began to pull out—her first visit to New York in four years, and the unhappiest in all her life. What the hell was the use of thinking back to the young punk from one of the dailies who had got her confused with Renée Adorée? What difference the wrong tables in restaurants and the inconveniently timed appointments at hairdressers and the night of sitting alone in her hotel room while a forty-dollar pair of theatre tickets went to waste? The benefit in Union City, New Jersey. The standup by Ken Englander, the aging architect, who had been glad enough in other days to get once around the floor with her at the Mayfair dances. The being made to wait on the telephone by the New York office of her agent, her own agent. The ruined Sophie dress and the lost earring at that South American's apartment. Why think of those things? Why not think of the pleasanter details of her visit?

Think, for instance, of the nice things that had been said about her on that morning radio program. Her appearance had been for free, but the publicity was said to be valuable, covering the entire metropolitan area and sometimes heard in Pennsylvania. Then there was the swell chat with Ike Bord, publicity man for a company she had once been under contract to. *"Whenner you coming back to us, Leda? . . .* Anything I can do for you while you're in town, only too glad, you know. I didn't even know you were here. Those bums where you are now, they never get anything in the papers." And it was comforting to know she could still charge things at Hattie's, where she had not bought anything in four years. And the amusing taxidriver: "Lady, I made you right away. I siss, 'Lydia Penley. Gay me an autograft fa Harry.' Harry's my kid was killed in the U.S. Marines. Guadalcanal. *Sure, I remember you.*" And, of course, her brother, who had come down all the way from Bridgeport with his wife, bringing Leda *a pair of nylons and a bona-fide cash offer* in case she had a clean car she wasn't using. The telephone service at her hotel had been something extra special because one of the operators formerly had been president of Leda's Brooklyn fan club. Through it all was the knowledge that her train fare and hotel bill were paid for by the company because she obligingly posed for fashion stills for the young-matron departments of the women's magazines, so the whole trip was not costing her more than eight or nine hundred dollars, including the visit to Hattie's. There were some nice things to remember, and she remembered them.

The train rolled through Lancaster County, and it was new country to Leda. It reminded her of the English countryside and of American primitives.

She got up and closed her door once, before washing her hands, but reopened it when she was comfortable. Traffic in the passageway had become light. The train conductor and the Pullman conductor came to collect her tickets and asked for her last name. "Leda Pentleigh," she said. This signified nothing to the representative of the Pennsylvania Railroad, but the Pullman conductor said, "Oh, yes, Miss Pentleigh. Hope you have an enjoyable trip," and Leda thanked him and said she was sure she would, lying in her beautiful teeth. She was thinking about sending the porter for a menu when the huntin'-shootin' type stood himself in her doorway and knocked.

"Yes?" she said.

"Could a member of Actors' Equity speak to you for a moment, Miss Pentleigh?" he said. He didn't so much say the line as read it. She knew that much—that rehearsal was behind the words and the way he spoke them.

"To be sure," she said. "Sit down, won't you?"

"Let me introduce myself. My name is Kenyon Littlejohn, which of course doesn't mean anything to you, unless you've *seen* me?"

"I confess I did see you in the station, Mr. Littlejohn. In fact, I almost spoke to you. I thought I recognized you."

He smiled, showing teeth that were a challenge to her own. He took a long gold case out of his inside coat pocket and she took a cigarette. "That can mean two things," he said. "Either you've seen me—I've been around a rather long time, never any terribly good parts. I've usually got the sort of part where I come on and say, 'Hullo, thuh, what's for tea? Oh, crom-pits! How jolly!' " She laughed and he laughed. "Or else you know my almost-double. Man called Crosby? Very Back Bay-Louisburg Square chap from Boston. Whenever I've played Boston, people are always coming up to me and saying, 'Hello, Francis.' "

"Oh, I've met Francis Crosby. He used to come to Santa Barbara and Midwick for the polo."

"That's the chap," said Kenyon Littlejohn, in his gray flannel Brooks suit, Brooks shirt, Peal shoes, Players Club tie, and signet ring. "No wonder you thought you knew me, although I'm a bit disappointed it was Crosby you knew and not me."

"Perhaps I did know you, though. Let me see—"

"No. Please don't. On second thought, the things I've been in—well, the things I've been in have been all right, mostly, but as I said before, the parts I've had weren't anything I particularly care to remember. Please let me start our acquaintance from scratch."

"All right," she said.

He took a long drag of his cigarette before going on. "I hope you don't think I'm pushy or anything of that sort, Miss Pentleigh, but the fact is I came to ask your advice."

"You mean about acting?" She spoke coldly, so that this insipid hambo wouldn't think he was pulling any age stuff on her.

"Well, hardly that," he said. He spoke as coldly as he dared. "I've very seldom been without work and I've lived quite nicely. My simple needs and wants. No, you see, I've just signed my first picture contract—or, rather, it's almost signed. I'm going out to California to make tests for the older-brother part in 'Strange Virgin.' "

"Oh, yes. David's doing that, isn't he?"

"Uh—yes. They're paying my expenses and a flat sum to make the test, and, if they like me, a contract. I was wondering, do you think I ought to have an agent out there? I've never had one, you know. Gilbert and Vinton and Brock and the other managers, they usually engage me themselves, a season ahead of time, and I've never *needed* an agent, but everybody tells me out there I ought to have one. Do you agree that that's true?"

"Well, of course, to some extent that depends on how good you are at reading contracts."

"I had a year at law school, Miss Pentleigh. That part doesn't bother me. It's the haggling over money that goes on out there, and I understand none of the important people deal directly with the producers."

"Oh, you're planning on staying?"

"Well . . ."

"New York actors come out just for one picture, or, at least, that's what they say. Of course, they have to protect themselves in case they're floperoos in Hollywood. Then they can always say they never planned to stay out there, and come back to New York and pan pictures till the next offer comes along, if it ever does."

"Yes, that's true," said Mr. Littlejohn.

" '*That* place,' they say. 'They put caps on your teeth and some fat Czechoslovakian that can't speak English tries to tell you how to act in a horse opera,' forgetting that the fat Czechoslovakian knows more about acting in his little finger than half the hamboes in New York. Nothing *personal*, of course, Mr. Little."

"Thank you," said Mr. Littlejohn.

"But I've got a bellyful of two-hundred-dollar-a-week

Warfields coming out and trying to high-hat us, trying to steal scenes and finding themselves on the cutting-room floor because they don't know the first thing about picture technique, and it serves them right when they find themselves out on their duffs and on the way back to their Algonquins and their truck-garden patches in Jackson Heights or wherever they live. God damn it to hell, making pictures is work!"

"I realize—"

"Don't give me any of that I-realize. Wait'll you've got up at five and sweated out a scene all day and gone to the desert on location and had to chase rattlesnakes before you could go to bed. Find out what it's like and then go back and tell the boys at the Lambs Club. Do that for twenty or fifteen years." She stopped, partly for breath and partly because she didn't know what was making her go on like this.

"But we're not all like that, Miss Pentleigh," said Littlejohn when she did not go on.

His talking reminded her that she had been talking to a human being and not merely voicing her hatred of New York. His being there to hear it all (and to repeat it later, first chance he got) made her angry at him in particular. "I happen to think you are, eef you don't mind. I don't care if you're Lunt and Fontanne or Helen Hayes or Joe Blow from Kokomo—if you don't click in Hollywood, it's because you're not good enough. And, oh, boy, don't those managers come out begging for us people that can't act to do a part in their new show. When they want a name, they want a movie name. Why, in less than a week, I had chances to do a half a dozen plays, including a piece of the shows. What good can New York do me, I ask you."

"The satisfaction of a live audience," he said, answering what was not a question. "Playing before a—"

"A live audience! On a big set you play to as many people as some of the turkeys on Broadway. Live audience! Go to a première at Graumann's Chinese or the Cathay Circle and you have people, thousands, waiting there since two o'clock in the afternoon just to get a look at you and hear you say a few words into the microphone. In New York, they think if they have three hundred people and two cops on horses, they have a crowd. On the Coast, we have better than that at a preview. A *sneak* preview! But of course you wouldn't know what that is."

"Really, Miss Pentleigh, I'm very glad to be going to Hollywood. I didn't have to go if I didn't want to."

"That wasn't your attitude. You sat down here as if you were patronizing me, *me!* And started in talking about agents and producers as if Hollywood people were pinheads from Mars. Take a good gander at some of the swishes and chisellers on Broadway."

"Oh, I know a lot about them."

"Well, then, what are you asking me for advice for?"

"I'm terribly sorry," he said, and got up and left.

"Yes, and I think you're a bit of a swish yourself," said Leda to the closed door. She got a bottle of Bourbon out of her bag and poured herself a few drinks into doubled paper cups and rang for the porter.

Presently, a waiter brought a menu, and by that time Leda

was feeling fine, with New York a couple of hundred miles and a week and a lifetime behind her. Dinner was served, and she ate everything put before her. She had a few more shots and agreed with her conscience that perhaps she had been a little rough on the actor, but she had to take it out on somebody. He wasn't really too bad, and she forgave him and decided to go out of her way to be nice to him the next time she saw him. She thereupon rang for the porter.

"Yes, Ma'am?" said the porter.

"There's a Mr. Entwhistle—no, that's not his name. Little-field. That's it. Littlefield. Mr. Littlefield is on the train. He's going to California. Do you think you could find 'im and ask 'im that I'd tell 'im I'd like to speak to him, please?"

"The gentleman just in here before you had your dinner, Ma'am?"

"Yes, that's the one."

"Mr. Littlejohn. He's in this same car, PA29. I'll give him your message, Ma'am."

"Do that," she said, handing the waiter a ten-dollar bill.

She straightened her hair, which needed just a little straightening, and assumed her position—languor with dig-nity—on the Pullman seat, gazed with something between approval and enchantment at the darkening Pennsylvania countryside, and looked forward to home, California, and the friends she loved. She could be a help to Mr. Littlejohn (*that* name would have to be changed). She *would* be a help to Mr. Littlejohn. "That I will, that I will," she said.

The Decision

The home of Francis Townsend could have been taken for the birthplace of a nineteenth-century American poet, one of those little white houses by the side of the road that are regarded by the interested as national shrines. In front of the house there was a mounting block and a hitching post, iron, with the head of a horse holding an iron ring, instead of a bit, in its mouth. These, of course, had not been used in the last thirty years, but use did not govern the removal of many objects about the Townsend place. Things were added, after due consideration, but very little was ever taken away.

The Townsend place was on the outskirts of the seacoast village, out of the zone where the sidewalks were paved. In the fall of the year and in the spring, the sidewalk was liable to be rather muddy, and Francis Townsend several times had considered bricking the path—not that he minded the mud, but out of consideration for the female pedestrians. This project he had dismissed after studying the situation every afternoon for a week. He sat by the window in the front room and came to the conclusion that (a) there were not really many pedestrians during the muddy seasons, since there were few summer people around in spring or fall, and (b) the few natives who did use the sidewalk in front of his place were people who had sense enough to be properly shod in muddy weather. Another and very satisfying discovery that Francis Townsend made was that few people—men, women, or children—came near his house at all. For a long, long time he had entertained the belief that the street outside was a busy thoroughfare, more or less choked with foot and vehicular traffic. "I am really quite alone out here," he remarked to himself. This allowed for the fact that he had made his study of the muddy-sidewalk problem in the afternoon, when traffic was presumably lighter than in the morning, when, for instance, housewives would be doing their shopping. The housewives and others could not have made *that* much difference; even if the morning traffic were double that of the afternoon, it still was not considerable. It was, of course, impossible for Francis Townsend to make his study in the morning, except Sunday morning, for Francis Townsend's mornings were, in a manner of speaking, spoken for.

Every morning, Francis Townsend would rise at six-thirty, shave and have his bath, and himself prepare first breakfast, which consisted of two cups of coffee and a doughnut. In the winter he would have this meal in the kitchen, cheerful with its many windows and warm because of the huge range. In the summer he would take the coffee and doughnut to the front room, where it was dark and cool all day. He would run water into the dirty cup and saucer and put them in the sink for the further attention of Mrs. Dayton, his housekeeper, who usually made her appearance at eight-thirty. By the time she arrived, Francis Townsend would have changed from his sneakers and khaki pants and cardigan to a more suitable costume—his black suit, high black kid shoes, starched collar, and black four-in-hand tie. He would smoke a cigarette while he listened to Mrs. Dayton stirring about in the kitchen, and pretty soon would come the sound of the knocker and he would go to the front door. That would be Jerry Bradford, the letter carrier.

"Good morning, Jerry."

"Good morning, Francis. Three letters an-n-nd the New York paper."

"Three letters and the paper, thank you."

"Fresh this morning. Wind's from the east. Might have a little rain later in the day."

"Oh, you think *so?*"

"Well, I might be wrong. See you tomorrow, in all likelihood." Jerry would go away and Francis would stand at the open doorway until Jerry had passed the Townsend property line. Then sometimes Francis would look at the brass nameplate, with its smooth patina and barely distinguishable name: "F. T. Townsend, M.D." The plate was small, hardly any larger than the plate for a man's calling card, not a proper physician's shingle at all, but there it was and had been from the day of his return from medical school.

He would go back to his chair in the front room and wait for Mrs. Dayton to announce breakfast, which she did in her own way. She would say, "Morning," as greeting, and nod slowly, indicating that breakfast was on the table. Francis then would take his paper and letters to the dining room and partake of second breakfast—oatmeal, ham and eggs, toast that was toasted over a flame, and a pot of coffee. Mrs. Dayton appeared only once during breakfast, when she brought in the eggs and took away the cereal dishes.

Francis Townsend's mail rarely was worth the pleasure of anticipation. That did not keep him from anticipating Jerry Bradford's knock on the door or from continuing to hope for some surprise when he slit the envelopes with his butter knife. The reading of his mail did, in fact, give him pleasure, even though it might be no more than an alumni-association plea, a list of candidates for membership in his New York club, or an advertisement from a drug or instrument company. Francis Townsend would read them all, all the way through, propping them against the tall silver saltcellar, and then he would take them with him to the front room, so that Mrs. Dayton could not see them, and there he would toss them in the fire or, in warm weather, put a match to them.

Then, every day but Sunday, Francis Townsend would take his walk. For the first thirty of the last forty years, Francis Townsend had had a companion on his walk. The companion always had been a collie; not always the same collie, but always a collie. But about ten years ago, when the last Dollie (all of Francis Townsend's dogs had been called Dollie) died, Francis Townsend read somewhere or heard somewhere that it took too much out of you to have dogs; you no sooner grew to love them, and they you, than they died and you had to start all over again with a new one. This bit of dog lore came at a time when Francis Townsend had just lost a Dollie and was suffering a slight nosebleed. It was not a proper hemorrhage, but it was not exactly reassuring as to Francis Townsend's life expectancy, and he did not want to take on the responsibility of another Dollie if Dollie were to be left without anyone to take care of her, any more than he wanted to go through the pain of losing another dog. Therefore, for the last ten years or so, Francis Townsend had taken his walk alone.

Although he would not have known it, Francis Townsend's daily—except Sunday—walk was as much a part of the life of the village as it was of his own life. The older merchants and their older children and older employees took for granted that around a certain hour every morning Francis Townsend would be along. Harris, the clothing-store man; McFetridge, the hardware-store man; Blanchard, the jeweller; Bradford, brother of Jerry Bradford, who had the Ford-Lincoln-Mercury agency—among others—took for granted that Francis Townsend would be along around a certain hour every morning. He had to pass their places on his way to the bank, and when they saw him, they would say, "Hello, Francis," and would usually say something about the weather, and Francis would nod and smile, and, without coming to a full stop, he would indicate that the comment or the prediction was acceptable to him.

His first full stop always was the bank. There he would go to Eben Townsend's desk and Eben would push toward him a filled-in check. "Morning, Francis." "Good morning, Eben," they would say, and Francis would put "F. T. Townsend, M.D.," on the check, and his cousin would give Francis three five-dollar bills. Francis would thank him and resume his walk.

At his next stop, Francis would sometimes have to wait longer than at the bank. Eventually, though, the barkeep would come to wait on Francis. "Hyuh, Francis," he would say, and place a quart of rye whiskey and a pitcher of water on the bar.

"Hyuh, Jimmy," Francis would say, and pour himself a rye-and-water. "Well, well, well."

"Ixcuse me, Francis, I got a salesman here," Jimmy might say. "Be with you in two shakes of a ram's tail."

"That's all right, Jimmy. Take your time. I'll be here for a while."

This conversational opening, or something very like it, had been fairly constant for forty years, inasmuch as the barkeep's name always had been Jimmy, since a father and a son had owned the business, or at least tended bar, during the forty mature years of Francis Townsend's life. Jimmy the father had discovered long, long ago that, as he put it, Francis was good for the entire bloody morning and didn't take offense if you left him a minute to transact your business. Francis was indeed good for the entire morning. If it happened to be one of Jimmy's busy days, he would remember to put four toofers—two-for-a-quarter cigars—on the bar in front of Francis before he left him, and Francis would smoke them slowly, holding them in his tiny, even teeth, looking up at the ceiling with one of them in his mouth, as though William Howard Taft or Harry Truman had just asked his advice on whom to appoint to the Court of St. James's. Francis never bothered anybody, not even during the years of two World Wars. He never tried to buy drinks for the Coast Guard or the Army Air Forces, and he was not a man whose appearance welcomed invitations on the part of strangers. Among the villagers—the few who would drink in the morning out of habit or temporary necessity—none would bother Francis or expect to be bothered by him. Francis had his place at the bar, at the far corner, and it was his so long as he was present. First-generation Jimmy and second-generation Jimmy had seen to that.

Each day, Monday through Saturday, January through December, Francis Townsend would sip his drinks and smoke his cigars until the noon Angelus from St. Joseph's Church. If he happened to be the only customer in the bar, Francis would say to Jimmy, "Ahem. The angel of the Lord declared, if I may say so."

"Correct, Francis."

Francis would take two of the three five-dollar bills from a lower vest pocket, and Jimmy would size up the rye bottle and pick up the money and return the estimated and invariably honest change. The tradition then was for Jimmy to say, "Now the house breaks down and turns Cath'lic."

"A rye, then," would be Francis Townsend's answer, in Francis Townsend's weak attempt at brogue. Whereupon Jimmy would hand Francis Townsend a wrapped bottle of rye and Francis would go home and eat the nice lunch Mrs. Dayton had prepared and take a good nap till time for supper, and after supper, when Mrs. Dayton had gone home, he would sit and read some of the fine books, like "Dombey and Son," the Waverley Novels, Bacon's "Essays"—the fine books in the front room—till it was time to bank the kitchen fire for the next morning and finish off the last of the wrapped bottle of rye.

That was about the way it had been with Francis Townsend from the time he finished medical school. That year, soon after his graduation, his uncle, who had raised him, said to him one day, "What are your plans, France?"

"First, I thought I'd interne at a hospital in Pittsburgh. A great many mines and factories out there and a man can learn a lot. Then, of course, I'll come back here and hang out my shingle. And I have an understanding with a girl in Philadelphia, Uncle. We're not engaged, but—we have an understanding."

His uncle got up and filled his pipe from the humidor on the mantelpiece in the front room. "No, boy," he said. "I'm sorry to say you can't have any of those things. You can never practice medicine, and you can't marry."

"Why, I can do both. I'm accepted at the hospital out in Pittsburgh, and the girl said she'd wait."

"Not when I tell you what I have to tell you. Do you know that both your father and your mother died in an institution? No, of course you don't know. There aren't many people in this village know. Most of the people my age think your father and mother died of consumption, but it wasn't consumption, France. It was mental."

"I see," said Francis. He stood up and filled his own pipe, with his class numerals in silver on the bowl. "Well, then, of course you're right." He took his time lighting up. "I guess there's no way out of that, is there, Uncle?"

"I don't know. I don't know enough about such things, putting to one side that I do know you shouldn't marry or you shouldn't doctor people."

"Oh, I agree with you, Uncle. I agree with you." Francis sat down again, trying to assume the manner of one Deke talking to another Deke in the fraternity house. "I wonder what I ought to do? I don't think I ought to just sit here and wait till I begin to get loony myself. There ought to be some kind of work where I couldn't do anybody any harm."

"You won't have to worry about money. I've fixed that at the bank. Give yourself plenty of time to pick and choose. You'll decide on something."

"Oh, very likely I will," Francis said. "I won't just stay on here in the village." But that, it turned out, was what he did decide to do.

Somebody Can Help Somebody

Sooner or later, Roger Casey was bound to run into Mrs. Deland; at the post office, the bank, the drugstore. He had been back a long time now, had his old job teaching in the high school, had had a rather successful season as basketball coach, and had been welcomed by just about every living soul in the village except Mrs. Deland. He had not consciously, deliberately been avoiding Mrs. Deland, but then when he saw her for the first time, getting out of her car in front of the post office, he got a slight stab of conscience: he should have gone to see her long ago. She did not see him, and he noticed that in the years since he joined the Navy, she had taken to using a cane. He resolved to make a point of seeing her—and kept putting it off until one day when he was in the bank and she came in.

"Good morning, Roger," she said. She switched her cane to her left hand and put out the right hand.

"Good morning, Mrs. Deland," he said.

"You look fine. Why don't you come and see me some time?" She spoke casually, as though she had not been particularly aware of his having been home all this time, or at least had not been offended by his failure to call on her. But Roger knew better.

"I've been intending to," he said.

"Come up any Sunday, Roger. I'm always home Sunday

afternoon, or you could drop in on your way home from the Mass." She always said "the" Mass.

"I'd like to, Mrs. Deland. How about this Sunday, if it's convenient?"

"Any time, Roger. You look very well." She smiled her goodbye, changing in mid-smile to a greeting for the teller.

That evening, Roger mentioned seeing her to his mother. "I ran into Mrs. Deland in the bank."

"Yes. Ran into her," said his mother. "I'd think it's been on your conscience, taking so long, without so much as a telephone call. She and the Judge were always good friends to this family, Roger Casey, and you especially. It wasn't a relation of ours that was here the first day after Mary died. It was Mrs. Boardman Deland—not because she knew Mary but because Mary was your wife. Mary she knew hardly at all, but it was a real lady with a real heart and love for you, *you*, that made Mrs. Deland put in her appearance, and with the weight of her own sorrow still on her."

"You told me. Anyway, I wrote to her when the Judge died."

"Yes, and the day she got the letter, she called me up to tell me so. 'What a considerate, gentlemanly thing for Roger to do, taking the trouble all the way out there in the Pacific.' Did she invite you up?"

"Yes."

"Then you go, and if you have some little souvenir, take it up to her."

"What, for instance? A Jap sword? The Army collected the souvenirs—we didn't."

"I didn't say a Jap sword. How about that muffler you gave me, made out of parachute material?"

"I gave that to you," said Roger.

"I know you did," said Mrs. Casey, softening. "Only I wish you did have *something* for her."

"Well—let me think. I'll give her a Navy cigarette lighter. She smokes."

"Very nice, very nice indeed. I'll wrap it like a present. I know where I have just the box for it."

"You don't have to," said Roger. "This is one I bought for Mary. It's still in the box."

Mrs. Deland received Roger on the sun porch, which, with its wicker furniture, gave the illusion of bright summer warmth even on a raw spring day like this one. Mrs. Deland reached for her cane, but Roger hurried to her before she could rise. "Roger, I'm so glad to see you."

"Thank you, Mrs. Deland. I'm glad to see you. Pleasure."

She sat back. "My, oh, my! You know, I think you look younger. You shouldn't, but you don't look over twenty-five, and you're almost thirty."

"Thirty next month."

"The twenty-eighth," she said. "This is one day I'm glad you came in the afternoon and not on the way from the Mass. I had some visitors, and I wouldn't have had much chance to talk to you."

Roger laughed a little. "There's no danger of me dropping in on the way home from Mass. I don't go to Mass."

"You don't, Roger? Since when?"

"Oh, over a year, I guess."

She paused, just a second or two. "I see," she said. "What are your plans? I imagine you've made all sorts of plans, but I haven't seen your mother in ages, so I haven't heard."

"Well, I'm back teaching."

"Yes, I knew that, but do you intend going on teaching? I should think that'd be pretty tame now. . . . I haven't offered you a drink. What would you like, Roger?"

"Bourbon, if you have it. Bourbon and soda or water, or any way."

"Would you mind helping yourself? Everything's there, or at least bourbon, scotch, rye, gin, that I know of. Give me some gin and ice in an Old-Fashioned glass, will you please? . . . Have you thought any more about studying law, Roger?"

"Sometimes."

"You don't sound—it isn't uppermost in your mind, is it? I still have the Judge's lawbooks. I kept them in case you might want them."

"Thank you."

"You're welcome, and you're more than welcome to the books. You know how the Judge felt about you, Roger. From the time you were a little boy."

"Yes, I do. I never knew why."

"Well, to be perfectly candid with you, I didn't at first. As far as I was concerned, you seemed to be a nice boy, and bright, but I couldn't see why you stood out. But the first summer we came here—I think you were nine or ten—the Judge liked you. I remember asking him why, particularly, and he said the way you cut the grass. He said you were thorough—thorough and honest. He'd sit right here with his lawbooks, when you didn't know you were being watched, and you'd go right on working even when you had no way of knowing anyone was looking at you. And you didn't skip the hard parts. If you couldn't get at the grass with the lawn mower, you'd use the sickle."

"I learned that at home. It was a habit."

"That, too. The Judge said you were properly brought up. He always noticed things like that. Little things."

Roger stood up. "I almost forgot, speaking of little things." He handed her the box. "Just a souvenir."

She opened the box. "A lighter. I don't own one. I've never owned a cigarette lighter. And this is from the United States Navy. Why, thank you, Roger."

"I meant to bring you some fluid, but the drugstore was closed. Sunday."

"I probably have some benzine in the kitchen."

She held the lighter tight, without looking at it, and for a moment there was no speaking, only the whistling of a breeze from the bay. Then she spoke, looking out at the bay as she began, turning to him as she went on: "I wish the Judge were here to help you, Roger."

He opened his mouth to speak, but only nodded. "He and I didn't know your wife very well, and she died before he did, so he was never able to tell me how *I* could have helped you."

It was here now, the moment with Mrs. Deland which he had been avoiding. With Mary's father and mother, and

even with his own mother, it had been their grief, their sad-
ness, as well as his own. But Mrs. Deland had not known
Mary, and what she would feel would be felt for him. And,
worse, he had nothing to offer her. "I guess nobody can help
anybody else in a case like that." It was his way of trying to
tell her not to expect anything.

"You're wrong, Roger. Here we sit, the bereaved. Me the
widow, sixty-eight, and you thirty, feeling just as old, and
both of us thinking, what's left for us?"

"That's right," he said.

"But it isn't. I can help you. I don't know exactly how, but
I can, because I'm happy. I'm not very lonely, because I
haven't very long to wait for whatever there is, but you,
young and healthy, you think you have a long, lonely life
ahead. Do you think that, Roger?"

"That's pretty much it, Mrs. Deland."

She got to her feet and stood at a window. He didn't know
what to do or to say, and then she turned and he saw that she
was weeping and must have been weeping while she looked
out the window. "I lied, Roger. I am lonely and I'm far from
happy. If it's only another day, it's still a long time, for me
or for you. The number of days doesn't count."

"No."

"Come and see me often, will you, Roger?" She sounded
amazingly young, as though her pleading were for something quite different. "Somebody can help somebody." She
was old, and what she felt for the Judge was very young.

"Yes," he said. He knew she wanted him to go. He stood

up, and as he walked out, he heard her say, "I don't know who, but somebody."

"I don't know who, either," he said to himself. "Nobody!"

The Pretty Daughters

The Major climbed in the company car and gave the driver the address. He put the attaché case beside him, stretched out his legs at an angle, and lit a cigar. At the exit gate the plant guard picked up the Major's pass and gave him a snappy non-reg salute, and the Major was on his way.

The night before and that morning there had been a heavy fall of snow. It had stopped now, but there had not been time to clear the streets, and the car's progress toward the city's residential district was slow. The Major was enjoying his cigar, the fact that soon he would be out of the Army, and the ride. It took him back to Christmas holidays twenty years ago when he would visit his classmates in cities like Hartford and Buffalo and Harrisburg. Once you got out of the built-up districts and into the sections where the houses were larger and had more ground around them, each anonymous house would hold a promise of fun. White house. Redbrick house. French type. Georgian type. Dutch Colonial type. Old Manse type. You didn't know who lived in any of them, but maybe in one of them, as you went from the station to the home of the people you were visiting, there would be a girl, a pretty daughter. Maybe at the very moment you passed her house she was out skiing or tobogganing, or maybe she was right there, taking a nap so she would look her best for the dance that night, the dances that occurred every night of your visit to these towns—Columbus, Reading, Binghamton. You never got to know much about the towns. If you did happen to drive a borrowed car, you were told where to go and how to get there, and "there" meant someone's house or the country club or the city club or the big hotel. You never stayed long enough to find your way about the town, and anyhow most of the driving was done at night, in a Packard or a Jordan or a Marmon or a Ford, with the side curtains flopping and the tire chains banging.

In the daytime if you went anywhere it usually was to someone's house three or four doors away, and you walked. You wore your coonskin coat and no hat and galoshes. You would time your arrival so that you would get there after the athletic ones who had been sliding down some hill. Everybody would drink a lot of tea and eat a great many watercress sandwiches. The girls would kick off their ski boots, which they wore whether they had been skiing or sitting around the country-club fireplace. The mother of the hostess of the moment would look in and there would be introductions and then she would depart, and presently the father would come home and beam on everyone, kissing most of the girls and making a joke about taking the boys to see the moose head in his den. The daughter of the house would pretend to be irritated. "Lord and *Tay*lor, Daddy! You'll have everybody fried before the Baldwins'." The boys would go to Daddy's den and have straight whiskey or ginger-ale highballs, and Daddy would shake up Orange Blossoms and take the shaker back to the girls. He would return to the den and politely inquire about the out-of-town boys' school

and family origins and then he would turn the job of barkeep over to his son, if any, or to a neighbor's son who had
the run of the house, and excuse himself to get into his tux
or full dress . . .

"Was that twenty-three thirty-eight, sir?" said the driver.

"I think so. Wait till I look." The Major opened his trench
coat and unbuttoned the top left pocket of his blouse. He
read from a slip of paper. "Twenty-three forty-eight," he
said.

The driver slowed down until the car was barely moving.
"I think this must be it. I don't see no number, but that last
was twenty-three thirty-eight."

"I think you're probably right," said the Major. "I'll get
out here."

"I'll go up and ask if it's the right house," said the driver.

"Will you? Fine. Thanks."

The driver went up to the porte-cochère, following car
tracks that obviously had been made hours before and in
which there were a few footprints. In a few minutes he was
back. "Yes, sir, this is it. They're expecting you. Major
Robb, the lady said."

"That's me," said the Major. He got out and gave the
driver two dollars. "I'll get a taxi from here. You needn't
wait."

He followed the driver's path and was knocking the snow
off his feet when the door opened, before he had rung.

"Come in, Major Robb. I'm Jean Reeves. Mother's around
the corner at a meeting and she told me to entertain you till
she got here."

"That's very nice of you," he said. He put his gear on a chair in the dark hall and followed the girl into a small, panelled room, in which there was a fire. The girl was quite tall and she wore a slipover and a cardigan, a tweed skirt, moccasins, a pearl necklace. He placed her age at twenty, but knew he must be wrong—she should be younger—and he was confused by her total lack of resemblance to Nancy, who beside this girl would be short and probably, by this time, sturdy. This girl had a superb, pared-down figure.

"I'd never know you were Nancy's daughter."

"I'm not. I'm her stepdaughter. She inherited me when she married Daddy."

"Oh, that explains it. I'm sorry your father's not here. I'd like to have met him."

"He had to go to Chicago this morning. I suppose Mother told you. We'll have tea when she gets here. Meanwhile, would you like something else? We have just about everything."

"I'd love a, uh, bourbon with a piece of ice in it," he said. "No fruit, no bitters, no sugar. Can you swing that?"

"That can be arranged and it's what I want, too." She opened a panelled door to a bar. He stood by the fire until she handed him his drink, and they sat down, facing each other, in front of the fireplace.

"Well, this is mighty pleasant. I was afraid your mother wouldn't remember me when I phoned."

"Well, frankly, she was quite surprised. But pleased, I can tell you that." She smiled. For the first time he noticed she was wearing a miniature Navy cap device.

"I see the Navy has moved in," he said.

"In a manner of speaking," she said.

"In a manner of speaking? Not married."

"Not married, but spoken for, in a manner of speaking."

"The Navy has good taste," said Robb.

"Thank you. And I'm glad to hear you say it, not only because of me, but don't you get tired of hearing the Army pan the Navy and vice versa? It's pretty silly."

"It is if you're fighting the kind of war I'm fighting. It doesn't make a hell of a lot of difference what color suit I wear. You can see by the absence of any ribbons that I haven't been using up much plasma."

"Well, you're a major, though."

"Even that's fairly recent, and I'm getting out pretty soon. I'm doing just about what I've always done, except I'm doing it for slightly less money. In civil life I'm a lawyer. I read contracts. In the Army I'm a lawyer, reading contracts. What about you, Jean? What did you do before the war? Paint, for instance?"

"Why did you happen to pick on that?"

"I used to know a girl in New York that looked a little like you. She was an artists' model and she painted."

"Oh, that's a relief. The kind of painting I've done wouldn't justify my looking artistic."

"Don't let it worry you. Even if I hadn't known the other girl painted, I would have guessed that you'd done some posing."

"I have a little, for Mother."

"Does she paint, too? I didn't know that. Of course, I

haven't seen her in fifteen years or more, so in that time she could have turned into a—a rodeo rider."

"That sounds a little disrespectful, but I'll let it pass."

"It isn't a bit disrespectful. I once knew a damned attractive rodeo rider. Very pretty, very intelligent, went to the University of Wyoming."

The girl nodded. "Mother did say you—you got around a lot."

"What did she *actually* say?" He smiled.

She hesitated. "Well, she said that if the term had been used in her day, you'd probably have been called a wolf."

"*Dear* Nancy. That's quite a build-up, isn't it?" He was annoyed.

"I think she's wrong about wolf."

"Why?"

She considered a moment. "Because wolf means predatory. I don't think Mother knows that. Wolf's a new word since her day. I think she thinks anybody that goes around with a lot of girls is a wolf. That isn't what wolf means, necessarily. A wolf—a wolf is out to make a score, just for the sake of the score. I don't think you're that."

"Thank you," he said. "You're not entirely right about me, but thank you."

"Why? Were you a wolf? Or *are* you?"

He studied his glass. "I've—I've done some howling on occasion. Put it that way. The fact is, I suppose your mother is justified. Shall I wait outside till your mother gets here?"

She did not answer, but got up and took his glass and filled it again, and her own with it.

"How old are you, Jean?"

"Twenty-three. Why?"

"I don't know," he said. He was suddenly unaccountably depressed.

She waited for him to go on, and when he did not, she addressed him rather too heartily. "What's come over you? Don't sit there making a long face."

"And don't you give me orders. Remember I'm old enough to be your father."

"And don't you pull rank on me, or age either."

"I can certainly pull age on you."

"Oh, no," she said. She put her hand over the Navy pin. "Do you think this stands for some twenty-three-year-old j.g.? How old are *you*?"

"Thirty-nine."

She laughed condescendingly. "A boy. This character is forty and a lieutenant commander."

"Maybe he's a *young* forty. I'm an old thirty-nine."

"You're both the same."

He realized that the time had passed for making jokes. "What did you mean when you said you were spoken for? I assume the gentleman is married."

"Very much married. Very *happily* married, probably, although he'd never admit it to me. Spoken for? I don't know what I did mean. I don't know why I said that, any more than I know why I wear this pin." She looked down at it and then very deliberately took it off. "I hope that will do some good."

"Maybe it will," he said, "if you want it to enough."

"Good God! If I want it to! He won't answer my phone calls. He's in San Francisco, but I know he's been East twice without looking me up or letting me know so I could go and see him. He's one of you New Yorkers. You probably know him. Nobody *here* knows him. Oh, he is *really* a bastard."

Her fury was exciting, but Robb did not know what to do next, or say. "We all are," he said.

"Yes," she said. She looked at him intently. "Why did you look up Mother after all these years?"

"In the neighborhood. Thought it'd be nice to see her again."

"No," she said.

"No?"

"No. You thought to yourself, 'Nancy lives in this town. Might be a good idea to look her up. She might not be too bad and it might be a very nice thing. A very nice thing.' That's what you thought."

He laughed. "You're exactly right. That's exactly what I did think."

"Of course it was. Well, Major Robb, you'd be disappointed, if I know you. She's completely domesticated, doing good works and not taking care of her figure. Oh, I can see your face when you get your first look at Mother. In fact, you're beginning to look that way now."

"I'll try not to any more," he said. He showed his teeth in a burlesque smile. "Is that better?"

"You have nice teeth," she said.

"Thanks. Listen, kid, do you want me to go?" When she did not answer, he went on. "You do, don't you?"

"No," she said.

"I ought to wait and say hello to your mother."

"I don't want you to go." She stood up and then seemed not to know why she had stood up. She looked at him helplessly and he got up and put his arms around her. She shut her eyes and kissed him, but there was nothing to it.

"I'm sorry, Jean," he said.

"I wanted you to kiss me."

"That isn't what I'm sorry about," he said. She looked down and away from him.

"You're sorry for me?"

"Yes."

"I'll say goodbye now," she said.

"All right," he said. She went out of the room and he heard her go upstairs, heard her moving around on the floor above, and again came that feeling of depression, but now, with it, the feeling that he was beginning to serve a sentence.

Everything Satisfactory

The status of Dan Schecter was such that he was as welcome, or was made as welcome, in a Hollywood night club when he came in alone as when he brought with him a party of twenty. Not that he ever had brought a party of twenty to the Klub Kilocycle. The Klub, which has been called the little club without charm, is a late spot chiefly inhabited by musicians and radio characters, and visited by picture people only when broadcasts draw them to the vicinity of Sunset and Vine. No such thing had brought Dan to the Klub initially. He dropped in that first night without quite knowing where he was; it was during the time when he was carrying that torch for Sandra Sardou, and he'd been drinking.

"Good evening, Mr. Schecter," the headwaiter said.

"Good evening," said Dan. "Why, it's Paul. Where the hell've you been, Paul?"

"Right here, Mr. Schecter. Five years. I own a little piece of the joint. You alone, sir?"

"Uh-huh. Didn't you use to be at the Troc?"

"No, sir. The Victor Hugo and Lamaze, remember?"

"That's right. Paul, I wanta sit down."

"Yes, sir." Paul took Dan to a table, transmitted the drink order—double brandy and soda—to a waiter, and, with his native tact, left Dan before either man got bored with the other. When Dan woke up the next morning he was in his own bed, alone, and his car was in the driveway, intact. This latter was a pleasant discovery, for he was fully clothed, and it was a matter of fairly common knowledge that when Dan woke up with his clothes on there was usually a wrinkled car downstairs, or no car at all. His lawyer had told him that it was becoming more and more difficult to square these motoring lapses. He examined the match books in his pockets, which vaguely recalled to him his visit, or the early part of his visit, to the Klub Kilocycle, and he remembered Paul.

Later that day he telephoned Paul, who told him that one of the boys had driven him home on orders from Paul. "You always used to take care of me, Mr. Schecter. It was nothing. Glad to do it, Mr. Schecter."

"How much do I owe you?"

"You signed a small tab, sir. Eleven or twelve dollars," said Paul. "And I gave the waiter five dollars to take you home. You understand I had to take the waiter off his station, so I had to give him something."

"I'll be in tonight or tomorrow, Paul. That was very decent of you."

It was three or four nights later that Dan went to the Klub for the second time, again alone. Sandra still would not leave the little nobody she was married to, although Isabel Schecter had walked out on Dan. Never had Dan managed such things so badly, and he was in the paradoxical situation of carrying a torch and losing his grip. He began to think of Paul as his only friend. He shook hands with him and in his hand was a fifty-dollar bill, which Paul glanced at as he led Dan to a table.

At that time the entertainment at the Klub was rather special but of a kind that Dan, who had owned a four-hundred-dollar set of drums in college, could appreciate. The eight-piece combination was for your listening pleasure and not intended to be danced to; the guitar, double-bass, and piano trio had made several recondite records; the blonde who sang with the band was known to every habitué, and Dan, watching her go to work, became aware that she was also known to him. He realized he must have been too drunk to notice her during his first visit.

"Paul," he said, summoning Paul. "Isn't that Mimi Walker?"

"That's right," said Paul, smiling.

"She looks wonderful," said Dan. "Tell her I'd like to buy her a drink."

Paul nodded, and when Mimi finished her songs he spoke to her. She turned in Dan's general direction and nodded, and in about five minutes she presented herself at Dan's table.

"Hello," she said. She seemed not to see that he had offered his hand and that his whole manner was of the friendliest. She sat beside him. "I'll have a bourbon and ginger ale."

"I didn't know you were here," said Dan.

"Come on, Dan. You didn't know I was anywhere. How phony can you get?"

"Do you think I'm a phony? I don't. A lot of things, but not a phony."

"Then don't start out as if you'd been—as if you had the Missing Persons Bureau out looking for me. I see where Sandra's still with her husband."

"Do you know her?"

"I was in a show with her. Oh, she's a lot younger than I am, but I used to know her, all right. She was always a lot smarter than I am. In fact, she still owes me some money on the Louis-Schmeling fight, and you know how long ago that was."

"She told me she was twenty-six."

"She could have been," said Mimi. "I mean she could have been sixteen when I knew her. That would make me thirty. O.K. I'm thirty. But you know better if you stop to think."

"You look wonderful," said Dan.

"Thanks."

"How long have you been here?"

"Five years," she said. "Since it opened."

"Oh."

"What do you mean, 'oh'?"

"I seem to remember Paul told me he's been here five years and owns a piece of the place. Is that how it is, Mimi?"

"For your information, I own a little piece of the joint myself. *Now* where are you?"

"Nowhere," said Dan.

"And that's exactly where you're going to get, Dan, so if you like the way I look, O.K., but just don't start thinking of a return engagement."

"You're a little ahead of me, but I guess that's what I *was* thinking."

"No!" She called the waiter. "Now I'll buy *you* a drink so you won't worry about the eighty cents it cost you to find out what you just found out. Give Mr. Schecter a double whatever he's having."

The waiter bowed respectfully. "The party on Five asked if you'll come over and have a drink with them, Miss Walker," said the waiter. "The one fella said he's a friend of Nat Wolff's."

"I'll be over," said Mimi.

"I know Nat, too, so don't go right away," said Dan, trying to be pleasant.

"Terribly sorry, chum, but I have to do another number."

"So soon? Well, I'll wait," said Dan.

She started to sing, "It'll be a long, long time." She got up and went to Table Five and spoke to the people but did not sit down. She went to the bandstand and sang a number and when she finished she went back and sat with the people on Five. Dan had a few drinks. He became aware of Paul standing near his table. How long Paul had been there, Dan had no way of knowing; he had been staring at the back of Mimi's head.

"Everything satisfactory, sir?" said Paul.

"I wouldn't go so far as to say that, Paul." He was on the point of asking Paul a question or two but decided against it for the time being. "We'll see how things work out."

Paul smiled. "Yes, sir."

The time passed. Dan clocked Mimi for six minutes at Table Five, and then when he thought it was six minutes more, it was over an hour more. Mimi would get up now and then and do a number and always rejoin the people at Five, and Paul would come around to Dan's table and smile and ask if everything was satisfactory. Dan's answers varied with the readiness of his wit. Somewhere along the line his drinks were being served in coffee cups, which, Paul felt he had to explain, was on account of The Law. The drinks went just as fast from coffee cups as they did from highball glasses, and they didn't have as much soda in them. On returning from a trip to the men's room, Dan hovered over his table unsteadily, glancing at the empty chairs and then at Mimi, laughing and talking at Table Five. Dan started to sit down, and if it had not been for Paul's help he would have missed the chair. "Thanks, Paul," said Dan.

"Everything satisfactory, Mr. Schecter?"

Dan laughed. "Goddam *un*satisfactory, but I said I'd wait and that's what I'm gonna do."

"Yes, sir," said Paul. "Tom, bring Mr. Schecter another drink." Dan and Paul grinned at each other.

The music stopped, had stopped without Dan's noticing, or noticing that he was the only customer in the place. He studied his watch without succeeding in concentrating on the position of the hands. "Paul!"

"Yes, sir."

"Am I the last one here? Where's Miss Walker?"

"She went home, sir," said Paul.

"Where does she live? Foolish question number five thousand two hundred and eighty." He gulped his drink and reached in his pocket and took out a money clip. He put two twenties on the table. "I'll give you twenty dollars more if you tell me where—no, *you* wouldn't tell me, you son of a bitch." He stood up and staggered to the street. Paul came up behind him and said to the doorman, "Mr. Schecter's car."

In a moment or two a boy drove the car around from the parking lot, and Paul went back inside the Klub and leaned against the bar. Mimi was standing there, and they both watched Dan getting into the driver's seat. She was frowning.

"I can't let him go like that," she said.

"You stay where you are," said Paul. "We'll read about him in the papers." The car roared away.

The Moccasins

About twenty people were sitting in the half darkness of the living room and the even darker screened-in porch, but the people were in twos and fours, conversing quietly or not at all, so it did not seem like a party. The gathering lacked the unity of noise that often goes with a much smaller group. It did have something else, which could have been an air of unified expectancy, or simple languorousness, or the two combined. Mary thought she sensed both, as though the people were just sitting around, lying around, waiting for something, but nothing in particular, to happen. It was late at night. The people were all—except for one woman —deeply tanned, and half of them could have got their tan from sports, which would account for their being tired. None of the men got up when Mary and her brother followed the Negro houseman into the living room. A portly man in an unbuttoned Hawaiian printed shirt was playing drums, using the wire brushes softly and expertly to the recorded music of the Dorsey brothers on the radio-phonograph. He was one of the brownest of all, down his chest to the khaki shorts and then again down his legs to his short socks. He flashed a smile and waved a wire brush in greeting, but went on playing without interruption, more interested in the tune, "Blue Lou," than in the arrival of Mary and her brother.

A stout, golden-haired woman, the only person not burned

by the sun, came up to greet Mary and Jack. Her smile was quick and polite and no more, implying that that would be all until the visitors identified themselves—and that if the identification were not satisfactory, the newcomers would be thrown right out.

"Mrs. Fothergill, I'm Jack Tracy, and this is my sister Mary."

The smile immediately warmed. "Oh, yes. Why, yes! I'm very *pleased*. Carl *Shepherd*."

"That's right," said Jack. He looked around, but in the dim light he could not recognize anyone. "He here?"

"No, he isn't. He isn't here *yet*, but he phoned from Hobe Sound. He's coming all right, and we're expecting you—my husband and I. Doc!"she called to the man at the drums.

He nodded in time with the music and spoke on the beat: "Com-eeng, Moth-thurr." The record ended and he joined the three. He moved quickly and with power that would not be good to run up against, but his gait was feminine. He waddled. Then immediately there was another contradiction—his hands were large and his grip was strong. He probably had been a capable guard in the late Hugo Bezdek or early Rockne era. His thin gray hair was parted in the middle and he looked as though he ought to be wearing a fraternity pin. His wife introduced the Tracys, and he put one hand on Jack's shoulder and the other on Mary's, which was bare.

"Carl'll be scooting in here any minute, but what's to keep us from a little libation? You name it, and we have it," he said. "There's a little thing of mine own called a Crusher." He grinned.

"Now, Doc," said Mrs. Fothergill.

"What's a Crusher?" Mary asked.

"You wouldn't want to try it and see, would you?"

"Maybe I'd just better have a Scotch," said Mary.

"Aw, no clients?" said Doc.

"Well . . ." said Mary.

"That's more like it," said Doc. "How about you, Mr. Tracy?"

"I think I'd better stick to bourbon-and-soda, sir," said Jack.

"Maybe you're right, if you've been drinking bourbon," said Doc. He chuckled. "I thought you were starting from scratch."

"*I* am," said Mary.

"Then, you come right along with Dr. Fothergill and learn how to make a Crusher. Mr. Tracy, you go along with *Mother*gill and give the ladies a treat." He put his arm around Mary and took her to a bar, which was on the porch.

"Fothergill and Mothergill, that's cute," said Mary.

He laughed. "I don't know who thought that up—at least, not in this generation. It's an old family joke, of course, back in West Virginia, where I come from, but they started calling us that, when we got married, in New York, too. Cannes. California. Down here. Whenever we meet a new crowd, sooner or later somebody'll get the idea of calling us Fothergill and Mothergill. Shanghai. India. Nairobi."

"You've lived everywhere," said Mary.

"Pretty near. Just about approximately everywhere—everywhere they'll have us," he said. He automatically but precisely mixed the drink during his chatter.

"This is a darling house," said Mary.

"It is that, all right. Frank and Hazel *really* know how to live."

"Who?"

"Oh, don't you know Frank and Hazel—the Blaylocks? You don't suppose this house belongs to us! No, child. We happen to know these friends of ours, and Hazel Blaylock broke her leg skiing up in the Laurentians, so they asked Mothergill and I to come down and open it for them, hold the fort till—now a little dash of Pernod. There. Yes, we keep it open for them till Hazel's leg heals, and, of course, much as we adore Hazel and much as I admire a pretty leg —well, we hope she takes good care of that leg for another month. Up north. That'll bring us right up to when we want to go to Palm Springs. There, take a sip of that and hold on to the top of your head."

Mary tasted the drink, putting a hand on her head. She smiled. "No effect so far."

"Of course not. I exaggerate a little, but it does have a wallop. Now your brother's, and one for Dr. Fothergill, and then you come over and sit with me." He made two highballs. As he was about finished, a man and a woman who had been talking earnestly in a far corner of the porch started for the door, which opened, Mary now could see, out onto a boat landing. A speedboat was tied up there.

"Hey, Buzz, don't go out there without a flashlight," Doc said.

"We know our way around," said the woman.

"Around each other," said Doc. "No, seriously—take a flashlight."

"Why?" said Buzz.

"Moccasins," said Doc. He reached under the bar.

The man looked at the woman and frowned. She shrugged, whereupon the man took the torch from Doc and they went out to the speedboat.

"If she feels that way about it, it must be love," said Doc. "Come on."

"Love could never get me to go out there," said Mary.

"Not at your age," said Doc.

Doc paused to give one of the highballs to Jack, who was sitting with Mrs. Fothergill and a couple—a young girl whom Mary had seen in New York and a second-rate movie actor, whom she had not noticed before. Then she and Doc went on inside to chairs near the drums.

"If you want to play, go ahead," said Mary.

"I will later. Just now I'd rather fan the breeze with you."

"All right," said Mary. "What did you mean about not at my age?"

They lit cigarettes before he answered. "At your age, love comes to *you*, and plenty of it, I imagine. You don't have to walk through moccasins for it."

"No?"

He studied her, then shook his head. "No." He waited a moment and then decided not to say what he might have been going to say. He swallowed half his highball before going on, and when he did, he returned to the chit-chat form. "Where do you usually go for the winter?"

"I've usually been in school."

"Good Lord, I knew you were young, but not that young. You probably came out this year."

"Last summer," she said.

"Last summer. Are you from Long Island?"

"Yes," she said.

"I smell money," he said. "Oh, sure. Your father is probably Herman Tracy."

"Yes," she said.

"Well, you've got nothing to worry about, except taxes, your head on a pikestaff, and stuff. Where does Carl Shepherd fit in? If I'm asking too many questions, it's because I always do. You're not related to Carl?"

"No," she said.

"That answers a *lot* of questions," he said.

"Does it? That's good," she said.

He smiled. "Don't be haughty with old Doc Fothergill. If I have your age right, I knew Carl before you were born, and if I haven't got it right, I'm only wrong by a year or so."

"Really?"

"Really," he said. "Now, I don't figure where your brother comes in." He looked out to the porch. "Well, now, maybe I do. In just this short space of time, he seems to be moving in on little Emily. Got that hambo from Hollywood talking to himself. I hope your brother can handle a sneak punch."

"How do you mean?"

"Well, our actor friend was doing all right with Emily before your brother got here," he said. "That's what I meant by a sneak punch. Mr. Hollywood's a bad actor, and I can say that again."

"Jack's a good fighter."

"Then that's settled. Maybe he belongs here," said Doc.

"Well, I should hope so."

"No, you shouldn't hope so," said Doc. The houseman took Doc's empty glass and Mary shook her head. Somebody got up and turned on the phonograph, which filled in the silence between Mary and Doc. She turned and saw that he was watching her. He smiled.

"Just beautiful, that's all."

"Thank you," she said.

"Not quite all. There's a lot of other things I'd like to know about you."

"Ask," she said.

"No. The things I want to know, you don't ask. You find out, but you don't ask. And it wouldn't do me any good to know anyway."

"No?"

The houseman handed Doc his drink. "No," said Doc. He drank deeply again, and looked slowly around the room and out to the porch. Two couples were dancing, the partners holding close to each other, and the conversations in the two rooms remained as subdued as when Mary had arrived at the party. Doc leaned forward and turned his head so that he faced Mary.

"Well?" she said.

"I'd give a year of my life to kiss you. Not a future year, mind you. One of the good ones."

"Would you?" she said.

"However, that's out of the question, for sixteen thousand reasons, so will you do me another favor?"

"I won't kiss you," she said.

"I have another favor. Will you please go home? Will you do me a favor and do yourself a favor and get out of here?"

"All right," she said, and started to rise. He reached out and touched her hand, but she pulled it away and went out to her brother. It took a minute to persuade him to leave, and Doc could not hear what words she used in doing it. When they came to the living room, Doc got up.

"I'll show you the way," he said.

"Thanks, we can find it," Mary said.

He walked with them to their car. "Tracy, I'd like to say one thing to your sister."

"My guess is you've said too much already. I probably ought to punch you in the nose, if I knew what this was all about."

"You don't, and anyway don't try it," said Doc. He spoke to Mary. "Just remember one thing. You don't have to walk through moccasins for it."

"What's he talking about?" said Jack.

"Oh, who cares?" said Mary.

Doctor and Mrs. Parsons

For a few weeks last summer, when the population of the village was trebled by the presence of the summer people, Doctor Parsons had been able to get a few hours' rest after evening office hours by calling on Joe Peck. Joe had a house near the beach, nowhere near the club, and he was a bachelor who lived with his sister. He lived there the year round, and the Pecks were not people to encourage casual dropping in by anyone they had not known thirty or more years. Dr. Parsons would stretch out on the sofa, unmolested by the telephone. That lasted until one night a desperate mother with a sick child took her car and drove along every street and lane until she spotted Doctor Parsons' car. After that the word got around quickly that if Doctor Parsons was not in his office in the evening you might find him at Joe Peck's house. The doctor's next scheme was to steal a nap in his car by parking behind the stable on the old Medbury property, which was practically abandoned and in disrepair. That was a good scheme for a while, and then one night Doctor Parsons was shaken gently by Harry Rossini, one of the village policemen. "Doc, we got a pretty bad accident. Three cars smashed up. One kid dead already."

"How'd you know where to find me?"

"Doc, I knew you been coming here over three weeks. I'd be for letting you sleep, but . . ."

"O.K., Harry." This time Doctor Parsons wanted to cry.

"I wouldn't of wakened you for a case of sunburn, Doc, you know that. But here we got two kids they're still pinned under one of the cars."

"I understand, Harry."

"One of them is my sister's kid. You know, Thelma."

"Oh, God," said Doctor Parsons. "Well, let's go. . . . Say, Harry, maybe you could fix up a place in the lockup for me two or three nights a week."

"I can do it. That's what I'll do. We got a cell."

September came, but the population did not thin out so much as in normal years. Many of the summer people had been unable to solve the apartment situation in town, and many others were waiting for husbands and sons to get out of the Army and have a real rest at their summer places. Quite a few talked about staying down all winter, and quite a few actually stayed: the Indian summer was extremely mild, and it was kind of fun to live in the partly closed houses, wear old clothes all the time, and have impromptu parties. It gave the young fathers a chance to get acquainted with offspring whom many of them were seeing for the first time but whom Doctor Parsons knew by heart. He was not very good about the babies' names or even the names of their parents unless he had known *their* parents. He would come back to his office with his pockets stuffed with prescription blanks on which he had written such notations as "Fat girl, about 24, living in Ed Rogers house. Child 16 months. Diphtheritic croup." It had long since ceased to embarrass him when he would call at a house and ask how the little boy was today and find that in this house it had been the cook who was his patient. It no longer bothered him in cases like that to read the expression in the eyes of the lady of the house (likely to be a modern young woman, medically knowledgeable), which accused him of drunkenness or at best senile incompetence. If they didn't like it, they could get another doctor. Of course, there was no other doctor; Jess Williamson had been in the Army for three years, and so had all the other doctors within a radius of twenty miles.

Doctor Parsons had a practice that thirty years ago would have been his dreams come true, but last summer and last fall and the winter before and the summer before that, he had tried to sell, with no takers. He had not been in a duck blind since the fall of '42, or to a lodge meeting, or a bank directors' meeting, or the get-togethers of the county medical society, where a man could get drunk without shocking the populace. He had had to fire the high-school kid whom he had hired as chauffeur: the kid wanted to take the Buick home nights. Mrs. Doctor Parsons, as everyone called his wife, told people that she was downright thankful when Rhoda, the cook, quit to work in a defense plant, even though it meant she had to do the cooking and the housework. At least, that gave her something to do besides try to keep the books straight with the doctor's pocket records. It occupied her hands during those many, many hours when she was completely out of touch with the only man in the world who had ever touched her.

She knew about the cell in the lockup which Harry Rossini had fixed up for Doctor Parsons. Harry had kept his promise, although his niece, Thelma's kid, never was unpinned from that mess last summer. The hideaway was no Waldorf-Astoria, but it was pretty nice: it was the lone cell for female lawbreakers in a community where no cell had ever been required for female lawbreakers. So far, the cell had been occupied only by a few favored drunks and by Doctor Parsons. The idea of her husband's sleeping in a cell did not appeal to Mrs. Parsons, but she reminded herself, as she had many times in the past thirty years, that a finicky woman ought not to marry a doctor.

You got finicky about things, but never *very* finicky. Never about things like his being shaved by the barber every single day but getting a haircut about the time the hair made him resemble Benjamin Franklin walking in Philadelphia, Pennsylvania, with a loaf of bread under his arm. Like his fancying up with a white linen weskit for a lawn party and then not changing the weskit because it was too much trouble to remove watch and chain, thermometer and chain, fountain pen, pencil, and other stuff that Doctor Parsons considered essential weskit equipment. Like his not getting a new pair of spectacles to take the place of a pair with one badly chipped lens. Like his not stopping just for one minute, sixty seconds, and writing down the actual name of the fat young woman whose sixteen-months-old baby needed twenty thousand units of antitoxin. If you had no children to worry about, wasn't it all right to worry about Doctor?

Doctor Parsons came home one day all beaming, all smiles. This was one day around Christmas time. He came in the kitchen door, which was unusual for him, because he usually came in through the side door, which gave entrance to the waiting room of his office. It was shortly after noon, and Mrs. Parsons had some vegetable soup on the stove and was reading the weekly paper. "Well," she said.

"Well, well, well," he said. "Three holes in the ground."

"What are you so full of beans for, all of a sudden?"

"Any calls?" he said, taking off his hat and overcoat.

"Any calls. What's the matter? You think you're losing your popularity? Seven or eight calls. They're all in on your desk. What on earth's the matter with you?"

"I may be losing my popularity any minute," he said. He sat on a kitchen chair and removed his arctics. "Jess Williamson's home."

"Jess Williamson?"

"He's home and out of the Army. He isn't even wearing his uniform. He looks fine, feels fine. Ready to go to work."

"*He* can't go to work so soon. Does he realize?"

"Now, now. He took final—I mean terminal leave and went to visit with his wife's family in North Carolina. Took it easy, played golf, et cetera, and now he wants to start making some money."

"Well, now, that's wonderful. When does he want to start all this?"

"Right away. I'm taking him around on my calls this afternoon. I told him he could have my office till he got established again. I even told him he could live in this house till he and his wife got settled. You and I could go away next week if we knew where to go."

"Personally I don't care where we go just so we go."

"That's the way I feel about it," said Doctor Parsons.

They went away, Doctor and Mrs. Parsons, to a New England city where the second-best hotel was managed by a cousin of Mrs. Parsons. They would sleep until nine or ten in the morning and have breakfast in their room. They saw a few old friends they had there when they wanted to, went to the movies in the afternoon when they felt like it, and when they were good and ready they packed up and went home.

When they got home, the first thing, naturally, that they did was to call the Williamsons, who by that time were back in their own house. Mrs. Williamson had seen to it that there were flowers to greet the Parsonses, and Mrs. Parsons called up to thank the younger woman. Doctor Parsons called Doctor Williamson to ask if everything was under control. Everything was, and Doctor Williamson was enjoying his practice. It was a bank-meeting day and Doctor Parsons felt free enough, for once, to go, and was pleased by the compliments of his fellow-directors on his healthy appearance. The second night home he went to a lodge meeting, where there were some irreverent remarks as to his not knowing the inside password (which of course he knew). By the end of the first week he had seen quite a few friends and acquaintances but he had not had more than ten or twelve patients. He wondered about this, and then discovered the explanation. Everybody thought he was still away. He thereupon got them to put an ad in the weekly paper: "Dr. L. W. Parsons has returned from out-of-town and has resumed his practice." The paper came out the following Friday afternoon, and Doctor Parsons was in his office early Friday evening. Although his evening office hours normally were from six to eight, he was there that night from six to nine, without a single patient.

He went back to the sitting room, where his wife was listening to the radio and sewing. "Quiet tonight," he said.

"Yes. What a relief!" she said.

"Quietest since—back before the war." He lit a cigar. "I think I'll take it easy from now on. With Williamson here, I'm not going to take any new patients."

"I was going to suggest that," said Mrs. Parsons. "I don't see why you should."

"I wouldn't like to put the whole load on Williamson's shoulders, but I don't see why I can't do a few more things I'd like to do. For instance, go to New York every two or three weeks, just overnight, and watch some of the good men operate."

"We could both go. Every other week you could go to a clinic and I could—shop, or take in a matinée. I think that'd be nice."

"The more I think of it the more it sounds like a good idea," said Doctor Parsons.

"I think it's a *very* excellent idea."

"Mm-hmm." Doctor Parsons picked up that week's *Time* and turned the pages for a few minutes. "Say, I was wondering. Don't you think we ought to have Williamson and his wife over for Sunday-night supper soon? He knows all the young people, but people like Reverend McKittridge and

his wife, and Lawyer Muldoon and *his* wife—he ought to
get to know those people better."

"Mm-hmm."

He returned to his magazine and read an article, or most
of it, then closed the magazine. "Want to play some cards?"

"All right," she said. "You get the table. By that time I'll
be done with my sewing."

He brought out the table and set it up and put the straight-
backed chairs in place. They sat down and he spread the
cards for the cut. She picked her card; he picked his and
held it out for her to see. He looked at her and saw that she
was not looking at his card but at him, and there was worry
in her eyes—worry, and almost pain. There was nothing for
him to do but to laugh.

"Who do I think I'm fooling, huh?" he asked. He laughed,
and now she smiled, too.

Wise Guy

Most of the people in the damn place were hacking away at their disgusting lunch, but I was still drinking Martinis and sitting alone in this thing that I guess could be called a booth, although it wasn't even the height of my shoulder. I had been there, I guess, about an hour, more or less, and I could see the people eating their lunch, and I could see out into the bar, where the people were two deep and making their purposeless noise. I said to myself I wish they'd shut up and go away, or at least sit down and be quiet. Their noise irritated me. They jabber-jabbered, babble-babbled away as if they had something to say, but none of them had anything to say. Those that came in together would blab-blab about what they were going to drink, and then, when they would order their drinks, they would have the same things they always had. Those that came in by themselves would light their silly cigarettes and bore the bartender with their phony politeness, just to prove to anybody at all that they knew the bartender. I hated them all. I had watched the first of them come in—those that came in together, and those who came in alone and were meeting somebody. I called the proprietor. "I'll bet you get goddam good and bored with these people, don't you, Frank?" I said.

"Well, yes an' no, Mr. Osgood," he said. He smiled and waved his menu and order pad.

"Oh, I know," I said. "They pay the freight. But seriously, don't you wish they were all in hell—me included?"

"Not *you*, Mr. Osgood. *You* know dat."

"I don't know anything of the kind," I said. "Since you're here, will you get me another drink, please?"

"Gladly, sir," he said.

I watched them all some more, and then of course when Frank himself brought me my drink, I had to go and spill it. "I bring you another right away, Mr. Osgood," he said. "That's all right."

"Of course it's all right," I said.

This time a waiter whom I did not know brought the drink, and I didn't spill this one. It didn't last very long and I didn't spill a drop. "You wish to order now, sir?" said the waiter.

"I do not wish to order now," I said. "I already told Frank I am waiting for a lady. How long have you *been* here?"

"Thank you, sir," said the waiter. He slapped the table with his napkin.

"When you get through with that imaginary crumb, will you bring me another drink, please?"

"Yes, sir," said the waiter. He got the drink.

I studied the terrible people, hacking away at their lunch, blab-blabbing, and I happened to look in the direction of the bar and saw Frank. He was grinning; I soon found out why. I looked away, trying to be as casual as possible but fixing my tie, the knot in my tie. I gave myself the proper time before looking again in Frank's direction, knowing that by this time he would be at my table. And he was. But he was not with the person whom I expected. He was with my kid.

"Hello, Father," he said. "I'm sorry I'm late, but I missed the train."

"Oh, you did?" I said. "Sit down." Then I remembered what I had completely forgotten. I was supposed to have lunch with him and take him and buy him a suit.

"I wouldn't of missed it, only I forgot the ad. I had to go back for it," he said.

"What ad? The suit ad?"

"Yes." He took a clipping out of the pocket of his plaid jacket.

"I know, I know," I said. "Do you want a coke or something? Did you have lunch?"

"No. Did you?"

"No," I said. "Do you want a coke? We're going to have to wait a while. I have an appointment with a lady that wants to buy a house. She ought to be here any minute."

"Oh. Then I will have a coke, please."

Frank had been standing there, listening to all this, and now he went to get the kid a coke.

I asked the kid: "How'd you happen to know I was here?"

"I went to the office, and I saw Miss McDermott just as she was leaving, and she told me you were here."

That was strange. McDermott usually had more sense. But she was right. All I had told her was that if anybody called, to be sure and tell them where I was. I guess she included the kid, or she may have thought I meant no one else but the kid.

"She said you left the office an hour ago. I'm sorry I'm late, Father."

"Oh, that's all right," I said. I picked up the ad and read it. It advertised the Prep Special, giving the price and details of the adaptability of the suit—how you could wear the coat with any pair of slacks, or you could wear the pants with a sweater or windbreaker. The kid's heart had been set on that suit. "The only thing is, I don't think I'll be able to go with you," I said. "This lady I'm meeting wants to buy—I told you that. But she's bringing her car and I'm going to drive out with her and show her the house."

"Oh," said the kid.

"I thought maybe something happened and you weren't coming in town, so that's why I made this appointment. You see?"

"Yes, sir," he said. He'd been getting out of the habit of saying "sir," so I was surprised. "Well then, I guess I better go."

"No, no, have your coke," I said.

"I don't want it," he said. "I wasn't thirsty, anyway."

I reached in my pocket. "Here, here's some dough. You're four dollars ahead on the deal. I'm sorry I can't go with you, but this is important."

The kid stood up and looked at the money, which I held out to him, and then at me, but he didn't look at me very long. "I'll tell Mother I didn't see you," he said. "She knows I missed the train." He started to leave.

"Now, wait a minute!" I said.

"Ah, never mind," he said. This time there was no stopping him. He was out of the place before I even got to my
feet.

Well, he was the one that wanted the suit. I didn't. The
little wise guy.

The Three Musketeers

Twelve people were asked for eight o'clock, and they were punctual. At about eight-thirty they went to the dining room and got their food and brought it back to the three bridge tables in the living room. Everyone knew everyone else, except this one girl, Jean Small. She was quite a bit younger than the others, and she, the only native New Yorker, felt rather out of it. All the others were from the same town, or the same county, in Pennsylvania, and the jokes and references were special and excluding, as her fiancé had warned her they would be. But the people were all nice to her, and Frank, her fiancé, had promised her that this would happen only once a year and needn't ever happen again if she didn't want it to. The time passed and the party was beginning to die, around eleven-thirty, and then some people came in who had been to the theatre. There were five of them—two couples and a man. Right away, before she got his name, Jean realized that the man was the Edward, or Eddie, who had been mentioned in tonight's jokes and Frank's earlier reminiscences.

Eddie was the only man who was not in evening clothes, but he was more dressed up than anyone else. Jean saw him as he came in the apartment; he stuffed yellow gloves into the pocket of his covert-cloth topcoat, and she noticed his Homburg, gray with a black band and white piping around the edge of the brim, the kind of hat you associate with race meetings and missions from England. He was smiling when he came in the living room and he got the reception he was expecting.

"Ed-dee!"

All the women were glad to see him and so were most of the men. He kissed all the women and shook hands with all the men. He was pleasant but unsmiling when he was introduced to Jean. He waited to hear her name and then said, "I wish you all the happiness in the world, and I certainly congratulate Frank. Frank, congratulations," and he again shook hands with Jean's fiancé.

As the only stranger in the crowd, Jean had been more or less guest of honor, but now there was no doubt about who was the Number One at the party. The host and hostess waited upon Eddie until he had his drink and cigarette. He sat down in the chair next to Jean, from which Frank had risen. "Oh, I beg your pardon, Frank, you sit here. This is your chair, isn't it?"

"Stay where you are, Ed," said Frank. Jean noticed, or could almost have sworn she noticed, an understanding flicker between two of the women. She was pleased and infuriated and confused, and especially was she infuriated by Frank, who was taking it as an honor that Eddie had usurped his seat.

Eddie was a big man, bigger than he should have been, because some of his bigness had to be fat. Nevertheless, he had muscular strength; she could tell that by looking at his hands, which made the oversize highball glass look small and fragile. If he crushed the glass, would he cut his hands? She thought not.

"I was glad to hear about you and Frank," he said.

"Why? You didn't know anything about me," said Jean.

"No, but I know Frank."

"Did you know his first wife?"

"Of course. I was an usher at their wedding," he said. "Nancy was all right. She just wasn't for Frank, that's all."

"How did you know I'd be all right for him?"

He was persistently pleasant. "Because he waited so long before getting engaged again. I know all about how he happened to marry Nancy. You know, we all grew up together."

"Yes, I know."

"We went to school together and the same parties and so on, but I was closer to Frank than anyone else except Joe. Joe Weems over there."

"Yes, I know which one you mean. I've heard about both of you."

"We were the three musketeers," said Ed.

"Did you call yourselves that?" she asked.

"Oh, now, you don't have to be sardonic, Jean. No, we didn't call ourselves that, but everybody else did. Understand, we *liked* being called the three musketeers, but we didn't make it up. It wasn't that kind of a friendship. All the fellows in this room belonged to a neighborhood club, or rather, fraternity. Omega Phi. 'Our Fraternity.' But Frank and Joe and I didn't have to have badges or anything like that. When we went away to prep school, we'd even write to each other, and that's unusual for boys. Later we used to go

out on dates together and get drunk together. After we grew
up, I was the first to come to New York, after I got out of law
school, and Frank and Joe stayed home for a few years and
Joe married Amy—you probably know all that."

"I do, but I don't mind hearing about *Frank*."

He looked at her and was on the verge of being angry, and
then he grinned. "I think maybe you've heard about me, too,
and I don't think it was all good."

"It was all very interesting. You're the big success in this
group, aren't you?"

"You mean money?" he asked. He nodded. "Yes, I guess
so."

"Well, isn't that what you wanted?"

"More than anything in the world, because I had less of it
than Frank or Joe. Not that my family were poor, but my
old man was a lawyer, not a very successful one, whereas
Joe and Frank were coal people, and where we come from
coal is king. Or was. Sure, I've made money."

"But money isn't everything," she said.

"Look, Jean, if you want me to go away, I'll go, but don't
keep taking these little digs at me. I like you all right and
there's no reason I can think of why you should dislike me.
Shall I move around with the other people or shall we start
again on a fresh basis?"

"Entirely up to you, but I don't want to monopolize you."

"Come on, Jean. I won't bite. Let's give it another start.
I'll tell you some more about Frank and Joe and me. Let's
see." He moved the glass around in his hands. "In some
ways, of course, Joe was closer to Frank than I was. As I told

you, they were coal people and their fathers and mothers saw a lot more of each other than they did of my father and mother. Joe's and Frank's families would go to Philadelphia and New York together and they had cottages near each other in Cape May. Cape May, New Jersey. A summer resort. We never quite made Cape May. Asbury Park one summer was the nearest we got, and that's not very near. That meant Joe and Frank had a lot of friends in common that I didn't know. Joe and Frank seeing each other the whole year round naturally made them closer, but when we were around sixteen, I think I was Frank's best friend. The reason for that was Frank and I could get dates but it wasn't so easy for Joe. Joe's no Adonis, half stiff the way he is now, but when he was sixteen he was even less so."

"I rather like Joe," she said.

"You certainly say that with finality. O.K., I'll go quietly." He got up, smiling, and she watched him lumbering, glass in hand, to a group of four. More intently, she watched the women as he joined the group, and knew that what Frank had said before they came to the party was probably true. "I'm not absolutely sure," Frank had said, "but I think Ed has had an affair with every girl that'll be there tonight, with the possible exception of Amy and *maybe* Lee."

Frank was telling a story to another group, and one of the women was at the piano, asking what she should play. Jean got up and went to the bedroom, where she had left her coat. She sat at the dressing table and took a long time putting on fresh makeup. She heard someone calling to the woman at the piano. "No, *not* 'Tell me, little gypsy.' 'Tell me why nights are lonesome.' " And they all began to sing.

Not quite all. In the mirror she saw a grinning face—Joe's. He came up and stood behind her, pushing against her.

"Hello," she said. "I think you're supposed to use the room down the hall."

He said nothing, but put his hands on her bare shoulders.

"Luck albaster," he said.

"Don't. What did you say?"

"Ya shoulders ur luck albaster. A, 1, a—" His hands slipped down her arms, and he leaned over and kissed her neck.

"Stop it, you damned fool," she said.

"Oh, parn me. Parn me. Wrong fella, huh? You waiting for Eddie?"

She stood up. "Brush the powder off your clothes, you fool."

"Joe." A woman stood at the door.

"All right, Amy. Com-ming, Mother."

Amy picked her coat off the bed and went out without speaking. Jean waited until she had heard them close the door of the apartment; then she walked slowly back to the living room and stood with the others around the piano, where she could face Eddie and give him what she hoped was a friendly, conciliatory smile.

It was Friday evening, the day the weekly paper was delivered, and Phyllis Richardson was going through it for mentions of herself. She had no trouble. On the front page she found three items of Page-One importance to the village and environs: Mrs. Valentine Richardson presided at the piano at the Eastern Star supper, which was given for the new members; Mrs. Valentine Richardson substituted for Miss Marianne Post, art instructor at the high school, during Miss Post's recent illness; Mrs. Valentine Richardson was among those present at the Norton-Williams wedding. Three items on Page One alone. Phyllis hummed as she turned to the third page. She was accompanied by the vast Cities Service Orchestra under the leadership of Paul Lavalle, since she possessed, like the modern child, the ability to concentrate while the radio was on full blast.

"Phyl, will you turn that down a little bit?"

"Hmm? What dear?"

"I'm trying to get some work done. Will you turn down the radio, not all the way, but we don't have to—"

"*I* know, *Val, dear*. We don't have to blow the side of the house out." She decreased the volume of the radio. The cabinet was closer to him than to her, but if he had turned it down to as low as he wanted it, he would not have reason to complain later, as he surely would do. She returned to her chair, the pleasure now gone from the three mentions on the front page; the pleasure of anticipation gone from the inside Personal Notes column. She sighed and lit a cigarette, humming no longer, leaving the singing to Miss Vivian della Chiesa, who was in a radio studio, appreciated, probably wearing a beautiful evening gown, earning two thousand dollars a week, soon going to a champagne supper on Park Avenue, where she would mingle with others who were famed on stage, screen, and radio.

Phyllis glanced about her, seeing nothing new, and nothing very old that she considered very good. The pictures of her class and Val's class at high school; her own class at the state teachers' college; the high-school football teams that Val had played on; the ship models that had been built by Val's great-grandfather; the brass bed warmer and candlesticks that had belonged to her own antecedents; the portrait-type photographs of her grandmother and grandfather; the small loving cups that Val had won in the 440 and 220; the furniture she had inherited, and the portable bar, resembling a barrel, which her friends and Val's had chipped together and bought for their wooden anniversary six years ago. Their last good party. She looked at Val and his fat back, hunched over his papers, with a dead cigar in his fat left hand and a thin yellow pencil in his fat right hand. That was a party, all right. At three-thirty nearly everybody had gone home but Bob and Edith Conforth, and Val and Edith went out to the kitchen to get some more ice, and when they came back, Val was wearing Edith's bra and panties and Edith was wearing Val's shorts and shirt. And Phyl and Bob stopped necking long enough to effect the same change. Only the four of them were left at the party, but Bob or Edith must have talked, or maybe it was Val, although he always denied he had. Anyhow, it got whispered around. Within a week the men who had left before three-thirty were stopping Phyllis on the street and saying, "Hey, Stingy, why didn't you ask *me* to stay the other night?" and some of the women, including two who had done some heavy necking of their own, stared at Phyllis as though she had burned down the orphanage. Val informed all who asked that the whole thing was exaggerated; he said he had put on Edith's hat and Bob had put on Phyl's hat. That was the story he had given at the bank when Ward Singer spoke to him. Phyl and Val never were sure whether Ward believed them or not. All Ward said was, "O.K., but if that story ever got to Old Lady Booth, your name is mud around here. I'd have to fire you, you know that." Yes, they knew that, all right, and it was what they had chiefly worried about. Old Lady Booth was the bank's principal stockholder. Fear of Old Lady Booth had made it certain that there had been no more parties like that one— hardly any parties at all. Six years of church suppers, ladies' auxiliaries, school activities, Val and his Scout Troop and air-raid-wardening, I   and her nurse's aid, Phyl and Val and their blood-doning, watching their step, saving pennies, getting no younger. She looked again at his fat back; you'd think he'd have lost some weight, all the blood he gave.

She picked up the paper again and turned to the third page and read the first item. "Huh," she said.

"What?"

"Mrs. Booth is back."

"Oh, God, yes. Good Lord!" He stood up as though his chair were electrically charged.

"What's the matter?"

"I forgot all about her," said Val. He took out his watch from one of the upper vest pockets. "I was supposed to go up and see her. Well, she usually eats pretty late."

"What do you have to see *her* about?"

"The usual stuff. Whenever she comes back from a trip, I always have to go and tell her how poor she's getting. Poor, my pratt." He started to button his vest and string the watch chain across his chest.

"I'm going with you," said Phyllis.

"No, I'll only be about a half an hour tonight. No use you driving up there twice for that short a visit. I'll just leave the car out in front of her house."

"I didn't mean that," said Phyllis. "I'm going with you and I'm going in the house with you."

"What are you talking about? You've never been in her house in your whole life."

"Well, I'm going tonight."

"You can't! What the hell's got over you all of a sudden? She won't let you in."

"Why won't she?"

"She just won't, that's all. There aren't five people in the whole township that can just drop in and pay a sociable call on that old battle-axe. When *I* go there, she doesn't even offer me a cup of coffee. You're coo-coo." He hesitated. "What do you want to go there for?"

"I want to see something. I want to find out something." She raised her voice. "I have my own reasons."

"Tell *me*. I'll find out for you. I'll introduce it in the conversation."

"I've made up my mind," she said. "You don't know where the keys of the car are."

"I'll walk," he said. He studied her. "What is it, Phyl? You're acting like a crazy woman."

"Are you going to take me?"

"Oh—all right," he said. "I don't know what I'll tell her. It's gonna be goddam embarrassing, I'll tell *you*. They'll hear about it at the bank tomorrow."

"*What* will they hear about? That you took your devoted wife with you when you called on Mrs. Booth. Is that awful? I always thought the bank—"

"All right, all right, all right," he said.

Mrs. Booth's butler was mildly astonished to see Phyllis. He had known her all her life and her father, the village veterinary, before her, but the question in his eyes was like that of a churchman seeing a staunch member of another faith going up the aisle. "Ho, good ebenin'," he said.

"Hello, Frank," said Val.

"Frank," said Phyllis.

"Yes, Ma'am. You just come right in sit down. I'll tell Missus ya here." There was a cold little room on the left of the door, to which Frank led the Richardsons without seeming to lead them. He accomplished this by not turning his back on them and not letting them walk past him. He saw them seated and went out to speak to Mrs. Booth.

"That's a surprised coon," said Val.

"All right. What if he is?" said Phyllis.

"She's not gonna see you, and I don't even know what you wanted to come here for. What shall I ask her?"

"Nothing," said Phyllis.

"Don't start lighting a cigarette."

"I will if I want to."

"Where are you going to put the ashes? What about the butt?"

"I'll swallow it. Oh, all right." There were no ashtrays in the room and no fireplace or other possible place for the disposal of ashes and butt. Phyllis put her cigarettes back in her bag.

"*Who?*" They heard Mrs. Booth's querulous voice from somewhere deep in the house, and Val nodded at his wife, as much as to say, "You see?" They sat silent until Frank reappeared. He grinned first at Phyllis and then turned away to speak to Val. She could not tell whether Frank was being arrogant under his friendliness, or friendly and nothing more. "You come back in the libr'y?" he said to Val, plainly excluding Phyl from the summons.

They left her alone in the cold little room, a room ideally suited to its present use, which was to receive the unwelcome. The lady of the house had left nothing in the room that would have added warmth or charm or beauty to any other room in the house. The two rugs were threadbare, the warped flooring rose and sank, the chairs were plush-covered and straight-backed, and the only picture was a representation of a mess of fish spilling out of an open creel. Across and down the hall a little way Phyllis could see a living room. The sliding double doors were open, and through them she could see a grand piano, comfortable chairs, and a large, comfortable sofa in front of a large fireplace. The library probably was to the rear of the living room, according to her guess, and the dining room probably adjoined the reception room in which she now stood, wondering what to do next. She was of half a mind to go to the living room, but changed her mind. She went back to her chair, and before she could sit down, she was startled by Frank's voice.

"Brought you the New York paper," he said. "They'll be a while, I guess."

"Thanks," she said. She took the wrinkled *Sun* and sat down.

"Guess you never been here before," said Frank.

"Never inside," said Phyllis. "Of course, I used to come to the strawberry festivals."

"Oh, yes, I remember. Yes, that was a good many years ago. You was just a little girl. Yes, they was a lot of work for me, them festibles. People messin' up the lawn with papers and trash. I didn't have old Tom Zarnicki gardenin' then. Had to do it all myself. I finally said to the Missus, I said, 'Send 'em a check and be done with it and don't have 'em messin' up my lawn with their trash and papers.' Tramplin' all over my flower beds. Cigar butts. I tell you, I was glad when the Missus put a stop to all that."

"Did you tell—does Mrs. Booth know I'm here?"

"No," said Frank. "Well, maybe your husband told her. I didn't. Did you want to see her about anything special?"

"No." She knew he was lying and that he had made known her presence.

"I didn't think so, so I didn't bother tellin' her you was here."

"Here, I don't want the paper," she said.

"Go ahead and read it. It'll help you while away the time."

"I don't *want* to read it," said Phyllis.

"We're all done with it. You ain't keepin' it away from anybody." He did not put out his hand for the paper. "Maybe I *better* tell the Missus you're here, in case your husband don't. In case she come out here and find you sittin' here, she don't know you by sight. I don't *think* she does. No, I *know* she don't."

"How do you know?"

"Because I remember her tellin' me she didn't know you by sight. She said she wouldn't reccanize you if she saw you."

"When did she say that? She wasn't expecting me or anything. Why would she say she wouldn't recognize me?"

"Oh, I'm speakin' of some years ago. When all that talk was."

"*What* talk?"

"Huh?"

"*What* talk? What talk some years ago?"

"Oh, you know. Four, five years ago. I'll tell her you're here."

"Never mind," said Phyllis.

He smiled. "Oh, yes. She'd be a mighty vexed woman if I didn't. I should of told her when you came."

"Well, why didn't you, then?"

"Why didn't I? Why, because we wasn't expectin' you, that's why."

"I never heard of that before," said Phyllis. "When two people come to a house, I never heard of a butler that announced one and not the other."

"No? Well, I'll tell you why. It's because I thought she wouldn't like it. I didn't want to say anything, but you didn't have to go ahead and accuse me of being a bad butler, so I'll tell you this much, Mrs. Richardson. I didn't say anything to the Missus because I didn't think she'd like you bein' here. Ixcuse me."

He left, and she waited, hardly breathing, trying to hear what would be said, but no words came to her. Ten minutes passed and a clock struck, and ten minutes more and the silence of the house was unbroken until she heard footsteps. She opened the paper as though she had been reading it, just as Val appeared in the doorway.

"Oh, that's good," he said. "You had something to read."

"Mm-hmm." She looked up and saw he was alone.

"O.K., let's go," he said.

On their way to the car, he half turned around and then said, "Well, you find out what you wanted to know?"

"What happened to the old lady?" Phyllis demanded. "Didn't she say anything about me?"

"Just said to say good night to you."

"*How* did she say it?"

"How? What do you mean how? She said good night, and for me to say good night to you. 'Good night, and good night to your wife.' That's all. Went up to bed. Why? What was this all about? Did you see what you came to see?"

"I found out what I wanted to know," said Phyllis.

He started the car. "Women's curiosity about other women's households," he said. "What *did* you want to know?"

"Women's curiosity about other women's households," she said. It was the truth, all right, only it wasn't the whole truth. *That* she had been deprived of for six years, and she began to wonder whether she wouldn't have been better off deprived of it for the rest of her life.

Val let her out at the front of their house, and when he came from the garage, she was standing in the middle of the living room. "I'm getting awfully sick of that barrel," she said.

Val laughed. "Oh-ho. One look at Old Lady Booth's place and you start doing our joint all over."

Malloy's friend, who had a Pontiac, drove him out to the address in the treeless dullness of Cambridge, Massachusetts.

"Here it is," said Malloy, reading the number.

"Here it is, all right," said the friend, "but it'd be a good idea to see if there's anybody home. You'll have one hell of a time getting a taxi from here."

Malloy got out of the Pontiac. The house was a multiple dwelling, maybe four, maybe six flats. In the vestibule he found the name he was looking for: Charles Van Buren. He pushed the button and a girl's voice said, "What is it?"

"This is James Malloy," he said. He was about to identify himself further when she asked him to wait a moment, obviously recognizing his name.

"Wait just a minute, please, Mr. Malloy," the girl said, for the second time. Malloy went back to the Pontiac, thanked his friend, said goodbye, and returned to the vestibule, carrying his bag. By that time the girl had the inside door open. "The clicker doesn't work," she said. "Will you come in?"

There was some mutual hesitation about shaking hands, with both deciding against it. He followed her into her apartment, which was on the same floor as the vestibule. He guessed with some positiveness that her delay was caused by her having to put on the sweater and skirt she wore. He

guessed with equal positiveness that there was nothing under-
neath the sweater and skirt, but this was of only passing
interest. She had a completely undisciplined fat figure, the
kind that a woman friend of Malloy's once had called the
truck driver's idea of Saturday night.

The living room, with the tired furniture, was dominated
by a baby's play-pen and, for contrast, portly tomes lying on
the little tables and the desk and chairs, because there was
no bookshelf.

"I expect Charles any minute," she said.

He liked her face. She had dark-brown eyes, a neat nose,
and a pointed first chin. Her hair was parted in the middle,
with a bun in the back. It was very dark brown and could
have used some serious attention.

"I guess I'm a little early," he said.

"No, no. I don't think so," she said. "Here, put your bag
—well, just put it anywhere. Would you like something to
drink? I'm afraid we can't offer much of a selection, but we
have some rye."

"No, thanks, Mrs. Van Buren. I don't want to interrupt
your household duties. I see you have a baby."

"That's all right," she said. "The baby's out for an airing
and I'm only too glad to sit and talk." She sat down,
smoothed her skirt over her knees, and straightened her
back, after the manner, possibly, of a dowager aunt. This
girl, Malloy knew, was a lady. She was nearly a generation
away from certain friends of his, but he was sure that if he
started the do-you-know game there would be a tumbling
forth of names: aunts and uncles, cousins and parents of

her friends. He was against that game as being a waste of time.

"You'll be happy to know, the car's all ready," she said. "After he talked to you yesterday, Charles went over to the garage and checked everything. He told them you were planning to drive to California right away. When you saw it two weeks ago there was something the matter with it. What was it? I forget."

"They were fixing the spare."

"That's right. Well, that's O. K. now. I think they—what do they call it?—rotated the tires. Moved the front one behind, and the behind one front or something. I don't know anything about it, but, oh, we loved that car!"

Malloy smiled. "I almost feel as if I were kidnaping your child."

"Oh, heavens no! Don't feel that way, Mr. Malloy. In *fact*, if you didn't take the *car* we'd almost . . ." Her eyes fell on the play-pen. She quickly lit a cigarette. "I was sorry I missed you when you were here the last time. We were hoping you'd come out and take pot luck with us. I may say my husband came home quite tight and full of stories about going to the Ritz with you and meeting some gorgeous creature from one of the shows. You're a writer, aren't you? I'm ashamed to confess I've never read anything you've written."

"The world is full of people that haven't read anything I've written. I'm a screen writer, Mrs. Van Buren."

"Oh, well that must be interesting too."

"It buys Duesenbergs," he said. "I'd rather be right here."

"Why? You didn't by any chance go to Harvard, did you?"

"No, I most certainly did not, or anywhere else. That's probably why I'd rather be here."

She laughed. "That *might* explain it."

There was a conversational gap which she closed. "Oh, let's have a drink. Don't be polite and refuse. Be polite and take one."

"All right, I will," he said. "Can I help you?"

"Sit still," she said. "There's only rye and ice, and soda or plain water. Or straight."

"With water for me, please," he said.

"Sure? We *have* soda."

"Sure, thanks. Plain water."

She brought the drinks, and by the color of them it was apparent that she had been sparing of the water. "Here's to your trip. Just think, starting out for California." They drank and she continued, "How long do you plan to take?"

"I haven't decided definitely. I'll go to New York tonight and make my plans from there. I'm going to take it easy. I don't have to be back for three more weeks."

"Wonderful. And you'll probably take the gorgeous creature along with you."

"Why, Mrs. Van Buren. What a thing to say! I can think of two reasons why I wouldn't do that."

"I can guess. Your wife and her husband."

"That's right."

She laughed. "And you'd rather trade *your* life for *here*. I *hardly* think so, really. I somehow can't imagine you pondering over the Rule in Shelley's Case."

"What *is* the Rule in Shelley's Case?"

"Some law thing. You have to learn it. That's all I know." She paused, listening to footsteps and someone whistling a dance tune. "That would be the next editor of the Harvard *Law Review*. We hope."

The apartment door opened. "Caught!" said Van Buren. "Hello, Mr. Malloy, I'm sorry I'm late. Hello, Baby." He tossed a green book-bag on a chair and shook hands with Malloy, patted his wife on the shoulder. He nodded solemnly at the drinks and at Malloy's suitcase. It was obvious that he was worn out, but trying to be jovial. "Drinking their heads off, bag packed, I suppose I'll find a note on the pillow."

"Yes, and look at the bag. Louis Vuitton," she said.

"Naturally it'd be a man with money," said Van Buren. There was no bitterness in the way he said it, but it was not the thing to say, and they all knew it. "How's for pouring me a slug of that?" he said.

The girl's eyes shone as she poured her husband's drink. She neglected to refill Malloy's glass, because now Malloy did not exist.

"I have the papers right here, Mr. Malloy, but let's have a few snorts on the Van Burens first. How is our child, my good woman?"

"Wonderful. No, as a matter of fact, she's sniffling, but I guess she'll live," said his wife.

"If I know her, she will," said Van Buren. He took off his jacket, which had suede patches at the elbows, and loosened his knitted black tie. The buttoned-down collar of his shirt was a little frayed, as though he had done an incomplete job with nail scissors. He sat beside his wife on the davenport. "Car's outside if you want to take a look, Mr. Malloy. We can go out in a minute for a thorough inspection."

Malloy looked out at the Duesenberg. "Say, that isn't the car I agreed to buy."

"Huh?" said Van Buren.

"Something new's been added. That spot."

"A spot?" said Mrs. Van Buren.

"A Lorain spotlight," said Malloy.

Van Buren laughed. "Oh, that. I'll tell you about that. I've had that ever since I owned the car but I never bothered to put it on. In fact I'd forgotten about it till I took the car to the garage for the check-up and the honest mechanic found it, so I had it put on. Maybe you don't like it. Some people don't like them because you have to drill the body."

"I like it fine but I'll have to give you another check. I have a certified check for the amount we agreed on. That spot—well, how much do you think?"

"Not a thing," said Van Buren. "Goes with the car."

"No, it doesn't," said Malloy. "I insist. That type I happen to know is worth around seventy-five dollars."

"I don't think it cost me that much."

At that moment Malloy chanced to look at the young wife and it was easy to see as she looked at her husband that she was thinking what seventy-five dollars would buy. "Will you take what *I* think it's worth?"

"Well, damn it, all right, I will," said Van Buren, smiling.

They watched Malloy as he wrote a check, and nobody spoke. He handed the check to Van Buren, who looked at it and handed it to his wife. He looked up at Malloy and nodded, without saying anything or smiling, but when she saw the check she smiled. It was for seventy-five dollars.

"You see, Mrs. Van Buren, you just can't get that particular type any more," said Malloy.

"Thank you," said Van Buren.

"Well, I ought to be pushing," said Malloy. "So while I have my pen out . . ."

"Right," said Van Buren.

The papers were signed and Van Buren, a considerably shorter man than Malloy, carried the suitcase as the three went out to the car. Malloy got behind the wheel and pressed the starter button. Hands were clasped, good wishes were exchanged, and the transaction was in general satisfactory.

Miss W.

Lights were out all over the building except in the hall-
ways and in Miss Woodberry's quarters on the first floor,
a two-room-and-bath suite that included her bedroom and
her study. This latter served also as an office. The door was
seldom closed while Miss Woodberry was in the suite, except when she had to give a girl hell or listen to a girl's more
serious problems. Tonight, she had a feeling, the door was
going to be closed while she gave a girl hell. Esther Bullock
not only was late; she had not even telephoned. The last girl
to check in had done so more than an hour ago. Traffic on the
highway, fifty yards down the driveway, had decreased to
the rate of one car every five minutes or so. It was still too
early to call the highway patrol. Miss Woodberry went on
marking papers, not fully concentrating on the job at hand
because Esther Bullock was on her mind. Her incomplete
concentration was not, however, inadequate; she knew what
to expect from each of the twenty girls whose papers she was
reading, and it was much too late in the year for genius to
make a sudden appearance. She did not even have to glance
at the names on those papers which were not typewritten;
she knew the handwriting. Indeed, she also could recognize
some of the typing and the type faces. Esther Bullock, for
instance, had a typewriter that had upper- and lower-case
caps.

Miss Woodberry lit a cigarette and moved her head in a circle and massaged the back of her neck. Esther Bullock was not doing herself a damn bit of good by keeping her from a hot bath and bed. It was better now to think of Esther as an inconsiderate little snip who was going to be punished, not as a bleeding figure under a wrecked car, or as a miserable creature being sick to her stomach, or as a precocious babe who was providing the ultimate in entertainment for that Yale boy who had taken her out. In the history of the school, now a junior college, only one girl had been killed in a motor accident, and that had been a long time ago, between Miss Woodberry's days as a student and her return as a teacher, so that, illogically, took care of that. As to the drinking, Esther did not drink. As to the other, Esther was a girl Miss Woodberry felt could take care of herself, and would.

She heard the thick-soled shoes of Harley, the night watchman, and then, at the door of her study, there was Harley himself with his watchman's clock hanging from his shoulder. "Still workin', Miss Woodberry?"

"Still at it," she said. She had decided not to mention the reason, for the time being. Later she might have to, but Harley was more of an old maid than most of the teachers and often had been suspected of carrying tales to the Dean.

"Going back to the kitchen, have m' lunch. If they's anything I can bring you. Some cold roast beef in a *sangwidge*. Small pot of *coffee*."

"Well, I think that'd be nice." She always gave Harley ten dollars at Christmastime. "Eat your lunch first." He'd be around again anyway, but what with eating his own enormous meal and fixing her snack he would be busy in the kitchen and not prowling around where he might see Esther. When he had gone she got up and put on her blazer. The thought of the hot coffee had reminded her that the night was cool and damp. In fact it was damp enough for skidding, and the roads in the neighborhood were narrow, with a high crown, and the ditches were deep. It would be quite possible to have a skidding accident. She called the highway patrol, and identified herself. "I'm sorry to bother you, Sergeant, but one of our girls is rather late checking in, and I was wondering, have you had any skidding accidents or anything like that?"

"No, we haven't Miss Woodberry. Not anything'd intarest you. It isn't so bad out for skidding. Do you want me to put it on the radio?"

"Oh, heavens, no. She's probably just—you know—late."

"Yes, Ma'am," he said, and she could feel him smiling. "I'll let you know, if we get anything."

That left out two possibilities: no accident, and if there was any dallying it was nowhere in this neighborhood; the cops had had their orders about that, direct from the Dean and her friend the governor of the state.

The telephone rang. It was the sergeant. "One of my men just called in. He was calling in about something else and I asked him did he have anything on like one of your girls, Miss Woodberry, and he did. Back on the River Road a '39 Chevvy coop went off the road into the ditch—"

"Oh, God!"

"But nobody hurt, so he's just making a routine report. Another party came along and they're taking the girl to the school. The young fellow owned the Chevvy's waiting for the tow car."

Miss Woodberry thanked him and made herself presentable for the Samaritans who were bringing Esther home. In about fifteen minutes she saw their lights in the driveway. The car drew up slowly. She stayed at her desk, but through the wide window she could see that it was a large, foreign-looking car and she could feel the vibration of the motor. Esther got out of the car and ran into the study.

"Oh, Miss W., I'm terribly sorry. We had a slight accident and we'd be there yet only, luckily, this friend of yours came along and stopped."

"What friend of mine?"

"That brought me home. He's parking the car out of the way," said Esther.

"He isn't going to be in anybody's way at this hour of the night." She heard a man's footsteps and then his voice.

"That's good," he said.

Esther stepped out of the way for him and for a couple of seconds Miss Woodberry looked upon a total stranger. "I'm sorry," she began, then she laughed. "Jim Malloy! Oh, no!"

"How are you, Amy?" They shook hands.

"Mr. Malloy can prove it, Miss Woodberry. We were so deep in the ditch, the road was higher than the car. We were there almost two hours and nobody'd stop for us except Mr. Malloy. Then of course that stupid cop came along. They're never around when you want them."

"That's a fact, Amy," said Malloy. "These kids are damn lucky to be alive."

"If it'd been on the other side of the road we'd of surely gone in the river."

"Are you sure you're all right?" said Amy Woodberry.

"Oh, sure."

"Very well. Report here after breakfast. Good night."

"But Miss W., Mr. Malloy's my witness," said Esther.

"You were overdue at it was, without the accident. Good night, Esther."

"Good night, Miss Woodberry," she said. "Good night, Mr. Malloy. Thank you ever so much for myself and Dwight."

"Glad I could help you out, Esther. I'll try some more," he said.

The girl looked from him to Amy and back to Malloy, raised her eyebrows almost imperceptibly, and left.

"Fancy seeing you *here*," said Amy. "How does that happen?"

"I made a wrong turn."

"I know, but why are you in this part of the country at all? I thought you lived in California."

"I do. I'm on my way there. I just bought that juggernaut outside, in Boston."

"What is it? I never saw one like it."

"It's a Duesenberg. How about a ride in it?"

"Are you crazy? Or do you think I am? Sit down and in

no time at all I'll give you a cold roast-beef sandwich and a pot of coffee."

"I'm down," he said. "So this is where you are. Didn't you go to school here?"

"Yes, and this is where I end up. Pretty thought."

"It agrees with you. You look fine."

"I look healthy. I'm fat as a pig, but so are you. I hardly recognized you. You ought to do something about it, Jim. I would have passed you on the street."

"I'd have whistled at you," he said.

"Would you? You haven't changed inside."

"Well, a matter of degree. By the way, that's a slick chick I just brought home."

"Now, really. You're old enough to be her father."

"But I'm not her father, so that makes it all right. Do me a favor. Go easy on her."

"Why should I?"

"For old times' sake," said Malloy.

"She was an hour late when she had the accident. She's my responsibility."

"For old times' sake."

"We were never anything much."

"Maybe you and I weren't, *much*, but you and somebody else were, and I took you to the doctor."

"Shut *up*, for God's sake!"

"All right. I just thought that was a nice kid, and when I realized it was you she had to report to, I figured she'd get a break. Well . . ." He started to rise.

"Sit down. I hear your sandwich and coffee," she said.

Harley hesitated at the door of the study, but came on in, raising his eyes only to study Malloy. He did not say "You're welcome" to Amy's "Thanks." Amy laughed. "Portrait of a Yankee about to start a little gossip about a middle-aged schoolmarm."

"I'd better go."

"No, let him have his fun. I have a spotless reputation. Eat your food."

"It's for you."

"It was, but I'm not hungry now."

"Eat half."

"All right, I'll eat half. I'll drink my coffee out of a glass, like a Russian." She got a tumbler from her bathroom and they commenced to eat.

"You can relax," she said. "I'll go easy with Esther." Her mouth was half full.

"Thanks," he said.

"But only for old times' sake," she said. "I haven't thought of those days for years."

"I don't believe *that*," he said.

"I don't either," she said. "Here we sit, fat and middle-aged, me chewing on one side of my mouth because I'm afraid of losing a filling."

"Right."

"It's not too bad," she said.

He said nothing.

She put down her sandwich. "Well, at least we can pretend it isn't."

"Right," he said.

The weather was fine, and that was the only thing Sam Derr could not have bought with money. He may have bought it with prayer; almost from the day Rosie announced her engagement, and certainly from the day she picked the date of her wedding, he had been saying, "God, I hope she has nice weather. Friday and Saturday, anyway." His prayer had been more than answered; it had been complied with. She had had nice weather all week, for all the parties, and the day of her wedding was all her father could have asked. The tennis court had been boarded over for dancing and there were large and small tables for the wedding party and the guests, and a tent for the buffet, open at the sides, and another for the bar, and the June afternoon was neither too warm for dancing nor too cool for sitting.

Sam wandered among the guests and he was not uncomfortable in his cutaway. He remembered names of many persons whom he never had seen until two or three days before and that made them think he was wonderful and made him think he was pretty remarkable too: school friends of Rosie's and of Frank's, and Frank's relatives. Fourteen ushers and the best man. Six bridesmaids and a matron of honor for Rosie. Sam remembered almost all their names. He stopped at a table here and a table there, carrying a Delmonico glass to sip from at the mention of how darling Rosie looked. He chatted with the leader of the orchestra, who had played for Rosie's coming-out party, and with the caterer, making a mental note to give them both surprise tips. He watched Rosie on the dance floor. It was her wedding day, to be sure, but she seemed even more popular than all the other brides he had seen. She would get scarcely a half dozen steps before someone would cut in. For instance, Sam saw her dancing with one of the ushers. He turned away to pick up a bottle to freshen the Delmonico glass, and when he looked again Rosie was dancing with young Jimmy Hayes, and Sam looked away long enough to put the champagne back on the table and she was dancing with Ben Gilbert. Ben was one of the very few natives who belonged to the yacht club, but he never danced. That was something, when Ben Gilbert danced. In sixteen years that the Derrs had been coming to this community he never had seen Ben Gilbert on the dance floor.

Ben moved along all right, too, the few steps he got. He was allowed to remain with Rosie a little longer than some of the others, because naturally he was older and was being treated with a certain amount of respect, and none of the ushers knew him. But for the time he was permitted with Rosie he moved along all right. When someone cut in he left the dance floor and went to the bar tent. Sam followed him.

He put his hand on Ben's shoulder, although Ben was a few inches taller. "I know where a fella could get some drinkin' whiskey instead of champagne," said Sam. "They pour champagne, no matter what you ask for."

"Well, I'm easily persuaded," said Ben. Sam took his arm and they went inside the house, to Sam's den.

"Now of course if you feel like champagne I have plenty of it here, on ice, but all the years I've known you I never heard you order it deliberately."

"No, I guess not," said Ben.

"Now I didn't mean anything by that, Ben. I just happened to think I never saw you drink anything but whiskey."

"I know what you mean, Sam."

Sam poured two stiff highballs in oversize glasses from a set of two dozen, each glass bearing a different etching of several breeds of duck. Sam handed Ben his glass.

"To Rosie," said Ben.

"To our girl."

"Well, hardly my girl, Sam," said Ben, laughing.

"In a way. You were the one taught her to sail a boat, which was more than I could do. Crabbing. Things like that. She always had a genuine fondness for you."

"Yes, I guess you're right. We always hit it off."

Sam sat down and pointed to a chair for Ben. "Let's see," said Sam. "Rosie was about eight years old the first year we came down here. That'd put you around—you'd have been about—"

"How long ago was it?"

"Sixteen years ago."

"I was twenty-six," said Ben.

"Oh, no, you must of been younger than that, Ben."

"I'm forty-two now, so I was twenty-six then."

"I thought you were younger than that. You looked

younger. Seemed younger. You do now. Never put on a pot belly and you never seem to lose your sunburn."

"Well, you know how it is," said Ben. "Being in the real-estate business in a place like this, it just about runs itself. Either things are slack and you can't force people to do business with you, so there's no use trying, or else like the past few years when they're begging you to rent or sell. Either way you don't need to spend much time in an office. No sense in sitting in an office when nobody'll be in to see you, and no sense sitting in the office when everybody's coming in to see you. So—why not go fishing?"

"Yes, I suppose that's why you Islanders all live to be a hundred. You have the right philosophy, but it'd never work for me."

"Why not, Sam? You have enough."

"Maybe I will, now," said Sam.

" 'Now'? You mean with Rosie married."

"That's right. I'd like to go away some place—I don't know where the hell to. California, maybe. Mildred and I. Play a little golf if we felt like it. Or Honolulu. Anywhere Mildred wants to go. She's entitled to a trip. You know she isn't Rosie's mother. Rosie's mother died twenty years ago."

"Yes, I knew that."

"Oh, sure you did. I guess Rosie told you just about every-thing."

"We used to have long talks," said Ben.

"Yes, she had great confidence in your judgment. 'Ben said this, Ben said that.' Mildred and I often commented on it, how Rosie'd prefer your company instead of the young fellows more her own age."

"Well, I guess I knew things that Rosie wanted to know, and it was easy to teach her." Ben spoke slowly and squirmed in the leather club chair. A silence came between the two men, and when Sam broke it, it was as though he were talking to himself.

"I looked at that little girl out there today, and earlier at the church, and I know what I did. I did what I've done all my life, from when she was just a tiny baby. Maybe I'm doing it now. At the office, or traveling, I'd find myself thinking of her, and then suddenly I'd stop thinking of her, but even though I'd stopped thinking of her there'd still be a smile on my face. I used to laugh about it. My partners caught on early. 'Sam's thinking of Rosie,' they'd say. People on trains, strangers, they must of thought I was an imbecile. I remember Willkie said to me, 'Listen, Derr, you're paying me a hell of a lot of *money* for what I've been telling you the last five minutes, but you haven't paid any *attention* at *all*.' So I had to tell Wendell L. Willkie about Rosie Derr.

"I guess I ought to be out there, but she'll be leaving soon." He looked at his watch. "Few minutes. I don't know where they're going for their honeymoon. I know in a general way. Canada. I don't want to know. Well, yes I do, but I wouldn't have wanted my father or mother telephoning me on my honeymoon." He stood up and took Ben's nearly empty glass out of his hand and poured two highballs. "To our girl, Ben."

"To Rosie," said Ben.

Sam smiled. "You don't have to be so careful, Ben. I know about you and Rosie."

"What *about* me and Rosie?" said Ben, angrily. "There *isn't* anything about me and Rosie."

"I know. That's *what* I know. But I've seen you look at her." Sam put his hand on Ben's shoulder, then looked again at his watch. "Time to go. But I wish you'd stick around and get drunk with me."

Ben stretched out his long legs. "I will," he said.

A Phase of Life

The radio was tuned in to an all-night recorded program, and the man at the good upright piano was playing the tunes that were being broadcast. He was not very original, but he knew all the tunes and the recordings, and he was having a pleasant time. He was wearing a striped pajama top which looked not only as though he had slept in it, but had lived in it for some days as well. His gray flannel slacks were wrinkled, spotted, and stained and were held up not with a belt but by being turned over all around at the waist, narrowing the circumference. On the rug in back of him, lined up, were a partly filled tall glass, a couple of bottles of beer, and a bottle of rye, far enough away from the vibration of the piano so they would not be spilled. He had the appearance of a man who had been affable and chunky and had lost considerable weight. His eyes were large and with the fixed brightness of a man who had had a permanent scare.

The woman on the davenport was reading a two-bit reprint of a detective story, and either she was re-reading it or it had been read by others many times before. Twice a minute she would chew the corners of her mouth, every four or five minutes she would draw up one leg and straighten out the other, and at irregular intervals she would move her hand across her breasts, inside the man's pajamas she was wearing.

The one o'clock news was announced and the woman said, "Turn it off, will you, Tom?"

He got up and turned it off. He took a cigarette from his hip pocket. "You know what the first money I get I'm gonna do with?" he asked.

She did not speak.

"Buy a car," he said. He straddled the piano bench, freshened his drink. "We coulda been up in the Catskills for the weekend, or that place in Pennsylvania."

"And tonight in one of those traffic jams. Labor Day night. Coming back to the city. And you could walk it faster than those people."

"But, Honey, we could stay till tomorrow," he said.

"I'd be in favor of that, but not you. Three nights away from the city is all you can take. You always think they're gonna close everything up and turn out all the lights if you don't get back."

"I like *Saratoga*, Honey," he said.

"Show me the difference between Broadway, Saratoga, and Broadway, New York. Peggy, Jack, Phil, Mack, Shirl, McGovern, Rapport, Little Dutchy, Stanley Walden. Even the cops aren't different. Aren't you comfortable here, Honey? If we were driving back from Saratoga tonight you'd be having a spit hemorrhage in the traffic."

"Fresh air, though," said Tom.

He kept straddling the piano bench, hitting a few treble chords with his left hand, holding his drink and his cigarette in his right hand. "Do you remember that one?" he said.

"Hmm?" She had gone back to her mystery novel.

"That was one of the numbers I used when you sent over the note. That was 'Whenever they cry about somebody else, the somebody else is me.' I was getting three leaves a week. The High Hat Box. Three hundred bucks for sittin' and drinkin'."

"Mm-hmm. And some kind of a due bill," she said.

"Uh-huh."

"And nevertheless in hock," she said.

"On the junk, though, Honey," he said.

"If you wouldn't of been taking that stuff it'd been something else."

"You're right," he said.

"Well? Don't say you aren't better off now, even without any three hundred dollars a week. At least you don't go around looking like some creep."

"Oh, I'm satisfied, Honey. I was just remarking, I used to get that three every Thursday. Remember that blue Tux?"

"Mm-hmm."

"I had two of them, and in addition I had to have two white ones. You know with the white ones, those flowers I wore in the button-hole, they were phonies. I forget what the hell they were made out of, but they fastened on with some kind of a button. They were made out of some kind of a wax preparation."

"I remember. You showed me," she said.

He put his drink on top of the upright and played a little. "Remember that one?"

"Hmm?"

He sang a little. " 'When will you apologize for being sorry?' I laid out two leaves for that. I liked it. Nobody else did."

"I did. It had a twist."

"The crazy one. Do you remember the cute crazy one? 'You mean to say you never saw a basketball game?' Where was it they liked that? Indianapolis."

"Yep," she said. She laid down the mystery novel, surrendering to the reminiscent mood. "I wore that blue sequin job. And of course the white beaded. Faust! Were they ever sore at me!"

"They loved you!" he said.

"I don't mean those characters from the cow barns. I mean the company manager and them."

He laughed. "Well, Honey, all you did was walk out on their show for some lousy society entertainer." He sneaked a glance at her. "I guess you been sorry ever since."

"Put that away for the night," she said, and picked up her mystery novel.

He played choruses of a half dozen tunes she liked, and was beginning to play another when the doorbell rang. They looked at each other.

"That wasn't downstairs. That was the *doorbell*," he whispered.

"Don't you think I know it?" she said. "Are you sure we're in the clear with the cops?"

"May my mother drop dead," he said.

"Well, go see who it is."

"Who the hell would it be tonight? Labor Day," he said.

"Go to the door and find out," she said. She got up and tip-toed down the short hall. He picked up the poker from the fireplace and held it behind his back, and went to the door.

"Who is it?" he called.

"Tom? It's Francesca."

"Who?" he said.

"Francesca. Is that Tom?"

He looked down the hall and Honey nodded. "Oh, okay, Francesca," he said. He stashed the poker and undid the chain lock and held the door open. In came Francesca, and her half-brother, Cyril, and a girl and a man whom Tom never had seen before.

"Is there someone else here?" said Francesca.

"No," said Tom.

"Honey's here, I hope," said Francesca.

"Oh, yeah," said Tom. "Come in, sit down." He nodded in greeting to Cyril.

"This is Maggie, a friend of ours," said Francesca, "and Sid, also a friend of ours."

"Glad to know you," said Tom. There was no shaking of hands. "These are friends of yours," he said, studying Francesca.

"Definitely. You have nothing to worry about," said Francesca. She sat down, and her half brother lit her cigarette. She was in evening clothes, with a polo coat outside. The girl Maggie was in evening clothes under a raincoat. Both men were wearing patent-leather pumps and black trousers with grosgrain stripes down the sides, and Shetland jackets. Sid's jacket was too small for him and most likely came out of Cyril's wardrobe. Francesca and Sid looked about the same age—late thirties—and Cyril was a few years younger, and Maggie could not have been more than twenty-one.

"I know we should have called up. We drove in from the country. But we decided to take a chance." Francesca liked being haughty with Tom.

"That's all right. It's quiet tonight," said Tom.

"I was going to *ask* you if it was quiet tonight," said Francesca.

"Yeah, we were just sitting here listening to the radio. I was playing the piano," said Tom.

"Really? Have you anything in the Scotch line?" said Francesca.

"Sure," said Tom. He named two good brands.

They ordered various Scotch drinks, doubles all, and Tom told Francesca that Honey'd be right out. He opened Honey's door on the way to the kitchen and saw that she was almost dressed. "Did you hear all that?" he said.

"Yes," she said.

"What do you want?"

"Brandy, probly," she said.

He continued to the kitchen, and when he brought back the drinks Honey was sitting with the society group, very society herself with Francesca and Cyril, and breaking the ice for Maggie and Sid. Sid was holding Maggie's hand, but Tom broke it up by the way he handed those two their drinks.

"Oh, Von said to say hello," said Francesca.

"Really? What's with Von these days? We didn't see Von since early in the summer," said Honey.

"He was abroad for a while," said Francesca.

"He's thinking of getting married," said Cyril.

"God help her, whoever she is," said Honey.

Sid laughed heartily. "You're so right."

"Is that the Von we know?" said Maggie.

"Yes, but no last names here, Maggie," said Honey. "Except on checks." She laughed ladylike.

Maggie joined up with the spirit of the jest. "How do you know Von isn't marrying *me*?" she said.

"The gag still goes. If you're gonna marry Von, God help you. But my guess is you aren't," said Honey.

"I'm not, don't you worry," said Maggie.

"I'm not worried," said Honey.

"I oughta rise and defend my friend," said Sid. He was still laughing from his own comment.

"Have you *got* a friend?" said Honey.

"You're so right," said Sid, starting a new laugh.

"I understand you're moving," said Francesca.

"We were, but we had a little trouble. I'll speak to you about that, Frannie," said Honey.

"Anything I can do," said Francesca.

"Or me either," said Cyril.

"Well, it's the same thing, isn't it?" said Honey.

"Not entirely," said Cyril. "Frannie has the dough in this family."

"Ah, yes," said Francesca. "But you go to the office."

They all required more drinks and Tom renewed them. When he served the fresh ones the seatings had been changed. Honey and Francesca and Cyril were sitting on the davenport, and Maggie was sitting on the arm of Sid's chair. They sipped the new drinks and Francesca whispered to Honey and Honey nodded. "Will you excuse us?" she said, and she and Francesca and Cyril carried their drinks down the hallway. Tom went to the piano and played a chorus. He turned and asked Maggie and Sid if they wanted to hear anything.

"Not specially," said Maggie.

"No. Say, Old Boy, I understand you have some movies here," said Sid.

"Sure," said Tom. "Plenty. You ever been to Cuba?"

"*I* have. Have you, Maggie?"

"No. Why?"

"Well, then, let's go easy the first few, hah?" said Sid.

"Sit over here and I'll set everything up. I have to get the screen and the projection machine. By the way, if you ever want to buy any of these—"

"I'll let you know," said Sid.

Sid and Maggie moved to the davenport and crossed their legs while Tom set up the entertainment devices. "You want me to freshen your drinks before I start?" he said.

"That's a thought," said Sid.

Tom got the drinks and handed them over. "You know

I have to turn out the lights, and some people prefer it if I keep the lights out between pictures. That's why I said did you want another drink now."

"Very damn considerate," said Sid. "When do we get to see the movies? Eh, Maggie?"

"I'm ready," she said.

The lights were turned off and the sound of the 16 mm. machine was something like the sound of locusts. The man and the girl on the davenport smoked their cigarettes and once in a while there was so much smoke that it made a shadow on the portable screen. Sid tried a few witty comments until Maggie told him, "Darling, don't speak."

In about fifteen minutes Tom spoke. "Do you want me to go ahead with the others?" he said.

"What about it, Kid? Can you take the others, or shall we look at those again, or what?" said Sid.

The girl whispered to him. He turned around. "Old Boy, have you got some place where we can go?"

"Sure," said Tom. "Room down the hall."

"Right," said Sid.

"I'll see if it's ready. I think it is, but I'll make sure."

He came back in a minute or so and stood in the lighted doorway of the hall and nodded. "Third door," he said.

"Thanks, Old Boy," said Sid. He put one of his ham-hands on Maggie's shoulder and they went to the third door.

Tom put the movie equipment away, and now that the lights were up he had nothing to do but wait.

The waiting never had been easy. As the years, then the months went on, it showed no sign of getting easier. The rye and beer did less and less for him, and the only time Honey got tough was if he played piano at moments exactly like this. He was not allowed to play piano, he *could* have a drink to pass the hour, but he could not leave the apartment because his clothes were in one room, and the little tin aspirin box that Honey did not know about was in another room. He was glad for that. He had fought that box for damn near a year, and lost not more than twice.

One of these days the thing to do was call up Francesca and get five palms out of her, just for the asking. Not spend it all on a Cadillac. A Buick, and wherever the horses were running at the time go there. What if Honey *did* get sore? What about giving up three leaves a week for her? And she'd always get along. What about tonight? Wasn't he ready to swing that poker for her? Where would Honey be if he let fly with that poker? Stepping over the body and on her way to Harrisburg, and leaving him to argue it out under the cold water with the Blues.

"What are *you* thinking about?"

It was Francesca.

"Me? I was just thinking," said Tom.

"Mm. A reverie," said Francesca. "What do I owe you?"

"Leave that up to you," said Tom.

"I don't mean Honey. I mean you," said Francesca.

"Oh," said Tom. "Including—"

"Including my friends," she said.

"Five thousand?" said Tom.

Francesca laughed. "Okay. Five thousand. Here's thirty, forty, forty-five on account. Forty-five from five thousand is five, four from nine leaves five. Forty-nine fifty-five. Tom, I never knew you had a sense of humor." She lowered her voice. "Tell Sid he owes you a hundred dollars. That'll make him scream."

"Sure."

"He has it, so make him pay," said Francesca. "He has something like two hundred dollars. Shall we wait for them, Cyril?"

"Oh, we have to," said Cyril.

"Here they are," said Francesca.

"Hundred dollars, Sid," said Tom.

"A what?" said Sid.

"Pay up or you'll never be asked again," said Francesca.

"A *hun*-dred *bucks!*" said Sid. "I haven't got that much."

"Pay up, Sid," said Francesca.

Maggie giggled. "I hope it was worth it," she said.

"Oh, by all means, but—am I giving the party?" said Sid.

"If you are you owe me plenty," said Francesca.

"I've some money," said Maggie.

"You know what that makes *you*, Sid," said Francesca. "Oh, Tom, I beg your pardon." She curtsied.

"Don't pay it then. Von never squawks," said Tom.

Sid took out his billfold and tossed Tom a hundred and twenty dollars and another ten. "Well, let's get the hell out of here," he said.

They all said good night to Tom and he to them. He

counted the money and was recounting it when Honey came in.

"We got any more beer in the icebox?" she said.

"Three or four," said Tom.

"I see one fifty, two twenties, and a lot of tens. It's all yours sweetie. For not going away to the country." She sank down in a chair. "You had a funny expression on your face when I came in. What were you thinking of?"

"Francesca."

She laughed a little. "Well, anyway I don't have to be jealous of that bum. The beer, Tommy, the beer."

He went to get the beer gladly. From now on the waiting would not be so bad.

The Chink in the Armor

Ted's first encounter with Mr. Wayne in five years or more took place one day last winter. Ted had come uptown for a business luncheon and was on his way to the subway, back to his office, when he saw Mr. Wayne, or, more accurately, a British Warm. He had had some notion of buying one while in the Air Forces, but other matters also had occupied his mind during those years and he had come home without one. The coat that Mr. Wayne was wearing had seen a lot of service, none of it military, but was in good shape. However, Mr. Wayne's *first* British warm had seen military service in World War I, when Mr. Wayne was with the Red Cross, and he had replaced it in the years of peace. Mr. Wayne also was wearing a tan cashmere scarf and a gray hat with the brim turned down all around, striped gray flannel trousers, white string gloves, and old brogues that had soaked up many's the half pint of Meltonian Cream. Mr. Wayne always looked as though he was just in from Unionville or Old Westbury for the day, seeing his solicitors before escaping to the life he knew and loved. The fact was that Mr. Wayne lived alone in a small flat on East Fifty-fifth Street and owned neither horse nor dog.

"How do you do, Ted?" he said. Mr. Wayne, without having a defined English accent, always gave off an elusive hah-ja-do sound to the words. Some people, who were not fond of Mr. Wayne, said his accent was actorish, but mothers of teen-age children said it was cultivated, not actorish. Educated. The accent of a man who still cared about the English language. "I say he sounds like that Cecil B. De Mille on the radio," one young person once said.

"Why, hello, Mr. Wayne," said Ted.

They shook hands. "I s'pose you're hurrying back to your office, but if I'm wrong I'd like very much to take you 'round to the club and buy you a whiskey."

"I'm sorry, sir, but I have to go back, all the way to Cedar Street."

"I'm sorry too. Still with your Uncle Frank, I gather."

"Yes, sir. If you're ever in that neighborhood—"

"Oh, I sh'll drop in, never fear. But why don't we ever see you at the club?"

"Oh, I don't know. When I go home on the subway I hate to get off just to have a drink there, and when I ride home with Uncle Frank we go up the East River Drive and that's too far over. Matter of fact, I've been thinking of giving it up."

"Oh, no. You musn't do that, Ted. Well, cheer'o, and do say hello to Frank."

They went their ways, Ted sharing his embarrassment with Mr. Wayne, both of them remembering that Ted never had written to thank Mr. Wayne for the money-belt he had given Ted when he joined the Army. Later in the day, on the way uptown, he mentioned the meeting to his Uncle Frank.

"How is old Chauncey? Not that he's any older than I

am, but I haven't run into him in years. He was one of those guys always hanging around the club twenty years ago, and I guess he still is. Never seemed to do anything. Never got drunk or anything. Always around in case you wanted somebody to have a drink with, or play bridge for small stakes. Then it was '29 and most of us had to get out and hustle. Didn't seem to alter old Chauncey's life, though. I'll bet if you add up the free meals that guy's put away in his lifetime . . . I'll bet he looks fine."

"Just the same."

"Yep. He oughta. Go to his apartment some time. He was a friend of your father's, and your mother's too. He was always incredulous that a lout like me could be her brother. Not that he ever said anything, but Chauncey's type can get those things across without saying them. You've never been to that apartment?"

"Nope."

"Go there some time. He's got every God-damn kind of hair oil and toilet water and bath salts—not that there's anything queer about Chauncey, but that's the way he lives. Everything's just so. He probably has about ten thousand a year without working, so why work? And of course he couldn't get married because he'd have to marry a girl with a potful of dough and at least the same social standing as he has, and that combination's pretty rare. The foreigners may not think so, but there aren't many things as smart as an American girl with a lot of money, and I guess they reasoned if they could have Chauncey for a meal or a week-end at Newport, why take him on for life? I guess he could have married money, but that wasn't all he wanted. Some time you get a look at that apartment. Family portraits. Swords belonging to his ancestors. Swords? He has a God-damn suit of armor! How far back do you have to go to find an ancestor that wore armor? The place looks like a men's club. Oak paneling, and I imagine that came from some manor house of the Wayne family. It's all authentic. I mean, fellows have told me it is, and you can usually tell anyway. It's all authentic but one thing, that is. Some years ago he was captain of a billiards team that went around playing clubs here and in Philadelphia and Boston. Well, up in his apartment he has a silver cigarette box and it's engraved 'To Chauncey Wayne, Captain,' and the year, and the names of the fellows on the team. Well, he bought that himself. I happen to know because I was on the team, and the last time I went to his apartment, and you can be sure it was the last time I was invited, he caught me looking at the box. Neither one of us said anything, but that gave me a lot of pleasure. He was a class ahead of me at Princeton and I was the dirt under his feet, especially during Bicker Week. If you ever go to that apartment I wish you'd take a look and see if he's still got it lying around." Uncle Frank laughed.

"The chink in his armor, eh?"

"Yep. Oh, hell, I guess Chauncey's all right. I never heard of him doing anybody any real harm, and you have to ad-mire a man that's consistent. Forty years ago he made up his mind how he wanted to live, and by God he's lived that way. That means he's a success."

"Oh, now wait a minute," said Ted.

"I don't mean by my standards, or yours, thank God."

Months passed with no mention of Mr. Wayne and little thought of him until Ted's telephone rang and it was Mr. Wayne.

"My dear Ted, Chauncey Wayne."

"Well . . ."

"You drop by my flat this ahfternoon?" said Mr. Wayne.

It was agreed, and Ted presented himself at Mr. Wayne's apartment. A surly Negro admitted him, and Mr. Wayne was awaiting him.

Mr. Wayne was wearing a blue blazer with some kind of pocket patch, and patent-leather pumps. "My dear boy," he said, "so nice of you to stop by."

"Not at all, sir."

Ralph, the valet, took Ted's hat.

"You'll have a John Collins and so'll I. Ralph?"

"Yassa."

Mr. Wayne nodded. "Now come you in, my dear boy. Cigar at this stage of the game? No? A pipe? Cigarette? Good show. Now then, my dear Ted—thank you Ralph. I'll ring. Now, my dear boy, how've you been?"

"Very well, thank you, sir," said Ted.

"Good," said Mr. Wayne. "I'll've a pipe. Not as a rule at this time, but tonight." He filled the pipe and tamped it. He took a long time preparing and lighting the pipe.

"Now then, what's the trouble? Please don't interrupt. My understanding is—I want to tell you how much I've heard. You really are in some gaff, aren't you, boy?"

"Well . . ." said Ted.

"I'll go right ahead like the bull in the china shop. It's a lady, and do you know, I can help. My experience. I haven't always been as old as I am now, you know. I lived in Paris two years, and that's not to mention New York."

"Oh," said Ted.

"Indeed, yes," said Mr. Wayne. "If these walls could talk, and thank goodness they can't. Now then, I get the apprehension you are in some trouble. Right?"

"In a way, sir."

"The, ah, lady in question—all hell's broken loose because of the lady in question. Yes?"

Ted nodded. "Far as I know."

Mr. Wayne laughed. "As far as you know. You may be sure. Now, my dear boy, I want you to have the benefit of my experience. The full benefit. This could be a turning point in your life. I know all about it." Mr. Wayne smoked his pipe and allowed his head to bob up and down, confirming his own judgment.

"Is that so, sir?" said Ted.

"It most assuredly is," said Mr. Wayne, with his head continuing to bob. "I know the husband in question."

Ted leaned forward and put out his cigarette. "I don't think so," he said.

"Please leave that to me, my dear boy. Her stupid husband'll talk to anyone that'll listen. Confidentially—I've never been able to stand the fellow, so I don't mind telling this to you—but confidentially, he's about to be warned."

"Warned?"

"At the club," said Mr. Wayne.

"Oh," said Ted.

"In which case, of course, he'd have to resign. I mean to say it isn't compulsory under the rules. A warning isn't a reprimand, and under the rules he wouldn't *have* to resign even if he got a reprimand, but anybody with any sense'd resign after an informal warning, or at the very least absent himself from the club for at least a year. A sort of voluntary self-suspension, you might call it."

"I see," said Ted.

"And of course only a damn fool would stay in the club after a reprimand, let alone a suspension, unless the suspension were for something like. . . . We had a case a few years ago. A member, one of the best, stole one of those luggage trucks, those two-wheeler things, you know, from one of the hotels in the neighborhood and wheeled it right into the club, right upstairs to the bar, and wouldn't part with it. Then when he was ready to leave he simply rolled it down the stairs. Those things are heavy, you know, and it chipped off the edges of all the steps. That little prank cost him a pretty penny and a year's suspension, but no one held it against him. A man should be able to hold his liquor like a gentleman, but this fellow'd been drinking in a strange speakeasy. Prohibition times, this was. And of course he hadn't hurt anyone, or given offense to anyone, so when his suspension was up he was welcomed back with open arms." Mr. Wayne chuckled. "Some of us did rag him a bit, his close friends, that is."

"Quite a caper," said Ted.

"You see the difference, don't you? I mean between my friend with the luggage truck, and this fellow, the husband of the lady you're interested in. J. B. I think we can refer to him by his initials. Ralph wouldn't be likely to know what we were talking about, and in any case he's very discreet. 'S had to be.

"Now this J. B. fellow," Mr. Wayne continued, "he sits around the bar making a bloody nuisance of himself. Both Mike and Jimmy have spoken of it to several of the older members, myself included, and those boys, you know, they're extremely patient. I've often said they're the real mainstay of the club, Mike and Jimmy."

"Tell you the truth, I don't know which is Mike and which is Jimmy, that's how often I go there."

"I *know* that, my dear boy, and it's a great pity, and that more or less leads up to what I wanted to talk about. My advice.

"You see, I recall your telling me you were thinking of giving up the club, and I've made a point of inquiring lately, among fellows your own age. Apparently you're still of the same mind. In the last week or two you told a friend of yours that it was a waste of money and so forth." Mr. Wayne stood up and leaned toward Ted. "My dear boy, you mustn't think of it!"

"Well, I—it seems like . . ."

"I know what you're going to say. You never use it, and you could use the money for something else, and so on." Mr. Wayne sat down again but continued to lean forward. "All that may be true, but my advice, from a wealth of experience in these matters, my advice is don't resign now! Whatever you do, don't resign now! Don't you see why?"

"Frankly, I don't," said Ted.

"Then I'll have to tell you why. This may be one of the most important decisions of your entire life. You see, dear boy, if you were to resign now it might seem to some of the members that you were resigning under pressure. That other fellow, J. B., he has one or two friends that don't know you, and they might get the impression that—well, you'd been given some strong hints to hand in your resignation. See what I mean? It'd be all over town in a week. Everybody in New York'd be saying Ted Crow was eased out of the Club, and you'd never to be able to live it down. If you lived to be a hundred there'd always be somebody'd remember that." He sat back in his chair and tapped a bell. The Negro appeared and without a word made two drinks, served them, and disappeared.

Mr. Wayne raised his drink. "Your health, sir," he said.

"Your very good health, sir," said Ted.

"Then there's another phase of this situation, and this proves what a great deal of thought I've given the matter. The value of experience. You see, if you were to resign now, you couldn't pick a worse time, because, remember what I told you? About J. B.? I'm almost positive he'll be getting his warning very soon. Matter of weeks. Maybe even days. And of course one thing I must say about him, he's been a member for so long that we'll have his resignation within twenty-four hours. He knows that much. *Then* if you want to quit, at least everybody'll know he quit first. I think you ought to wait a year, but at any rate hold off until the end of the next quarter."

"It's sort of like giving J. B. a pistol with one bullet in it and telling him he knows what to do."

"In a manner of speaking, yes. Yes, it is something like that," said Mr. Wayne.

Ted paused, looking at his drink. "Naturally, Mr. Wayne, I have my own opinion of him, but do you really think he'd be damn fool enough to resign under those circumstances?"

"I think he'd be a damn fool not to. He's enough *not* a damn fool not to, not to refuse to resign, if I make myself clear," said Mr. Wayne.

"I know what you mean. Yes, I guess he would. Resign, I mean."

"Oh, anyone would, really," said Mr. Wayne. "But I want you to promise me you're not going to, at least for three or four months."

"All right, and of course I want to thank you for taking all this trouble."

"If I had a son of my own I could only wish somebody'd do the same thing, and I know if I had a son, your father would have given him the same advice. Or your Uncle Frank, for that matter. He's a man of the world, but of course very busy, and I don't imagine he knows anything about the situation."

"I hope not. He hasn't said anything. Speaking of Uncle Frank, he told me one time about this apartment."

"Oh, really? I'd forgotten he'd ever been here. Yes, of

course he's been here. Years ago. Would you like to take a look around?"

"By all means."

"I'll have to send you on your way in just a bit, because I'm dining with some people in Gracie Square, but I'm always happy to show off this old place." For the next five minutes he provided instruction and entertainment of a historical nature, all having to do with objects in the living room. "Then this is my dressing room. Nothing of interest here." There was a kidney-shaped desk and on it a silver cigarette box, but Mr. Wayne did not lead the way into the room. "That about does it," he said. He was obviously trying to guess whether Ted had seen the silver box, and if so, whether the box meant anything to him. He held out his hand and adroitly led Ted to the hall door. They made their farewells and Ted went home.

Conversation in the Atomic Age

Malloy, the occasional writer for motion pictures, and Mrs.
Schmidt, his Los Angeles society friend, had said all they
had to say; that is, Malloy had said his say, which was to report the news of his wife and family back East and provide
whatever information he possessed on their few mutual
friends in New York and Philadelphia. That had taken him
up to the salad, which, contrary to California custom, was
served after the entrée. Malloy had known it was going to
be that way, but taking her out to dine and dance was a duty
that Malloy performed because Mrs. Schmidt was always
nice to his wife. When he had finished, Mrs. Schmidt took
over. Her monologue was entirely predictable, involving, as
always, her full report on every party she had been to in the
last three weeks, including the names of people Malloy
never had heard of, what some of the women wore or did not
wear, who was sleeping with whom, how the people came by
their money, and Transportation. Mrs. Schmidt was fascinated with Transportation, and her stories always went
something like the one she plunged into that night. "I drove
the Cadillac to Santa Barbara," she said, "because Gil Foster had left his car there, at Hopie and Jack's, and then Jack
and I came back together in his Buick because he had a
meeting downtown and wanted to use his car, and then of
course Hopie, she was coming down that afternoon and so

she drove my car and Gil had to come down alone, too, in his car. You know that old Lagonda he has."

"No, I don't know Gil Foster."

"Oh, I thought you did. Of course you do. Gil Foster? From Tulsa? Part Cherokee? Or maybe Choctaw. Terribly rich and terribly attractive."

"Nope."

"Hmm. Well, anyway, he has this old Lagonda he bought before the war. He's always kept it out here for when he visits here. He likes an open car but Martha won't ride in one, but of course she hardly ever comes to Los Angeles. She isn't very attractive."

"Is she part Indian?"

"I don't know. Why?"

"I just wondered."

"What made you ask that? Did you hear she was? She might be. I don't really know very much about her. They had an apartment here one winter, at the Town House, but she didn't make the grade. Nobody liked her, but I don't think it was because she's part Indian. After all, Gil is, and everybody's crazy about Gil. And you know, you coming from the East, you don't understand—"

"Now, listen, you're from Schenectady, New York."

"I was *born* there is all. Except for when I was at St. Margaret's I've lived here all my life, so I consider myself an Angeleno and I understand the Western point of view about Indian blood. All my friends out here have some Indian blood, at least all the oil crowd, or most of them. It's no disgrace."

"Oh."

"I'm rather surprised at you taking that attitude. I thought all you New Dealers were all for marrying Jews and Negroes and Hottentots all over the place."

"Oh, no. Just giving them a quart of milk every day."

"Huh?"

"It's all right."

"Oh, I get it. You're kidding me. I never can tell when you're serious or when you're kidding. How does Kate put up with it?"

"Christ knows."

"She's darling. Everybody loves Kate. She's rather hard to get to know. Reserved, I mean, and not very talkative, but I've heard an awful lot of people say how attractive they thought she was. You know you're awfully lucky."

"Am I?"

"What do you mean 'Am I'? Don't you think you are?"

"I was trapped into that marriage."

"What do you mean you were trapped into that marriage? That's the most conceited statement I ever heard you make. How do you mean you were trapped?"

"Kate was seven months pregnant when I married her."

"Why, you—I don't believe it. Whatever happened to the baby if she was pregnant?"

"I'm sorry, but that's a secret."

Mrs. Schmidt studied Malloy. "Are you telling me the truth?"

"No."

"I didn't think you were. I didn't fall for it. Oh, there's your friend Ed Vanralt. Who's he with?"

"Bee Corson."

"Bee Corson. Rex Corson the actor's wife? They broke up, didn't they?"

"Mm-hmm."

"Why? Did she leave him or did he leave her?"

"I don't know."

"You know the Corsons, don't you?"

"Not terribly well. Her only very slightly."

"Call them over."

"What for?"

"I'd like to talk to them. I think Ed Vanralt's very attractive. Does he still go around with Joan Lord in New York?"

"I suppose so."

"You know, for a writer you aren't a bit interested in people, are you? . . . She's plastered."

"Looks that way, but of course she may have diabetes. Orange juice'll fix her up."

"How long has she had it? Rex Corson must be a bastard to leave her just when she gets diabetes. At least wait till she dies."

"She may hang on for years."

"I feel sorry for her. . . . You're wrong. She's drinking double Scotches. The waiter just poured two Scotches in the glass and hardly any soda. She hasn't any diabetes. She's just plastered. I thought Ed Vanralt was Rex Corson's best friend."

"He is."

"Then what's he doing out with his wife?"

"That's a hard question."

"Not to me it isn't. Look at her patting his cheek."

"I can't look."

"Oh, stop. Just because Ed Vanralt's a friend of yours you don't have to put on an act. Those two'll be in bed in an hour if I know anything."

"Well, it *is* getting late. What are *your* plans?"

"I don't know. What would you like to do?"

"I'd like an early quit tonight."

"So would I. I tell you, you don't have to take me home. I left my car in the Brown Derby parking lot. You take me there and I can get home all right from there. Except, I just happened to think. Marge is stopping for me in her car tomorrow, we're going to Pat's luncheon. I think it'd be all right to leave my car in the parking lot all night or else put it in some garage in the neighborhood. Then I could go to the luncheon with Pat and she could take me to the garage after we've had our fittings. We're both having fittings after Pat's luncheon but then Pat is driving to Palm Springs after our fittings and I want to have my car because I'm going to Attie's for cocktails but I'm leaving early because I have to dress for dinner. Gil has a new Oldsmobile with the hydromatic shift. I don't mean Gil, I mean Arthur. And he's stopping for me around eight. So it might be a better idea if I left my car in Beverly. That is, if you don't mind taking me home."

"Not a bit," said Malloy.